"I'm Not Thinking About Your Twin Or The Game Or The Money, Shannen."

He cupped her cheek with his hand.

Reflexively Shannen closed her eyes and leaned into his hand, letting the warmth of his palm envelop her. If she intended to tell him to leave, this was the time to do it, a small voice inside her head counseled.

"How can I think of anything else but you?" His voice was a low, seductive growl. He curved his other hand over her hip in a firm, possessive grasp.

Shannen's eyes stayed closed. She didn't want him to go, she achingly admitted to herself.

"Everything is so…unfinished between us, Ty," she whispered.

"I think it's time we altered that, don't you?" Ty trailed kisses along the curve of her jaw. When his mouth finally, lightly brushed hers, she exhaled with a hushed whimper. It was all the invitation he needed to deepen the kiss. Shannen felt desire and urgency erupt inside her with breathtaking speed.…

Dear Reader,

Wondering what to put on your holiday wish list? How about six passionate, powerful and provocative new love stories from Silhouette Desire!

This month, bestselling author Barbara Boswell returns to Desire with our MAN OF THE MONTH, SD #1471, *All in the Game*, featuring a TV reality-show contestant who rekindles an off-screen romance with the chief cameraman while her identical twin wonders what's going on.

In SD #1472, *Expecting...and In Danger* by Eileen Wilks, a Connelly hero tries to protect and win the trust of a secretive, pregnant lover. It's the latest episode in the DYNASTIES: THE CONNELLYS series—the saga of a wealthy Chicago-based clan.

A desert prince loses his heart to a feisty intern in SD #1473, *Delaney's Desert Sheikh* by award-winning author Brenda Jackson. This title marks Jackson's debut as a Desire author. In SD #1474, *Taming the Prince* by Elizabeth Bevarly, a blue-collar bachelor trades his hard hat for a crown...and a wedding ring? This is the second Desire installment in the exciting CROWN AND GLORY series.

Matchmaking relatives unite an unlikely couple in SD #1475, *A Lawman in Her Stocking* by Kathie DeNosky. And SD #1476, *Do You Take This Enemy?* by reader favorite Sara Orwig, is a marriage-of-convenience story featuring a pregnant heroine whose groom is from a feuding family. This title is the first in Orwig's compelling STALLION PASS miniseries.

Make sure you get all six of Silhouette Desire's hot November romances.

Enjoy!

Joan Marlow Golan

Joan Marlow Golan
Senior Editor, Silhouette Desire

Please address questions and book requests to:
Silhouette Reader Service
U.S.: 3010 Walden Ave., P.O. Box 1325, Buffalo, NY 14269
Canadian: P.O. Box 609, Fort Erie, Ont. L2A 5X3

All in the Game

BARBARA BOSWELL

Published by Silhouette Books
America's Publisher of Contemporary Romance

To Irene Goodman and Joan Marlow Golan,
whom I'd never vote off the island.

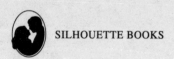 SILHOUETTE BOOKS

ISBN 0-373-76471-5

ALL IN THE GAME

This edition published by arrangement with Harlequin Books S.A.

® and TM are trademarks of Harlequin Books S.A., used under license.
Trademarks indicated with ® are registered in the United States Patent
and Trademark Office, the Canadian Trade Marks Office and in other
countries.

Visit Silhouette at www.eHarlequin.com

Printed in U.S.A.

BARBARA BOSWELL

loves writing about families. "I guess family has been a big influence on my writing," she says. "I particularly enjoy writing about how my characters' family relationships affect them."

When Barbara isn't writing and reading, she's spending time with her *own* family—her husband, three daughters and three cats, whom she concedes are the true bosses of their home! She has lived in Europe, but now makes her home in Pennsylvania. She collects miniatures and holiday ornaments, tries to avoid exercise and has somehow found the time to write over twenty category romances.

One

"**E**verybody ready to shoot another day in paradise?"

Tynan Hale, chief cameraman for the reality game show *Victorious,* assembled his crew for their daily briefing before heading from their camp across the island to the contestants' camp.

"Paradise? Come on, Ty, no need to sugarcoat things for us. We all know what we're really shooting is the seventh circle of hell," kidded Reggie Ellis, a junior cameraman.

The crew snickered appreciatively. Ty grinned, too, though he guessed he probably shouldn't encourage such irreverence toward the show and its contestants.

The Powers That Be—the network suits, the show's creator, the sponsors, virtually everybody connected with *Victorious*—viewed their project with a seriousness usually reserved for nuclear weapons. No jokes or humor there.

Ty found the job of trailing around contestants on an island, hour after hour, filming their every word and action, to be sometimes interesting and/or irritating and/or dull, but hardly a matter of the gravest concern.

No wonder he would never be a member of The Powers That Be. Not only was his attitude all wrong, his family already had been there, done that.

And failed spectacularly. The family downfall had been such a public sensation that not a day went by without Ty Hale pausing to relish his current anonymity.

He paused to relish it now, while he and the crew loaded their equipment onto the boat to take them to the *Victorious* contestants' camp. Here he was, Ty Hale, chief cameraman, good at his job but essentially a nonentity. It wasn't the standard dream come true, especially in the entertainment industry, but it was certainly his.

And it was the name Hale that made it all possible. Changing his surname seven years ago—unofficially, though not legally, because *that* would've drawn attention to it—was the smartest move he'd ever made.

If anyone in the media were to know that he was actually Tynan Howe, son of the notorious former congressman Addison Howe, a member of the infamous Howe clan…

It wouldn't happen, Ty assured himself, for possibly the millionth time. The contestants were the attraction and sole focus of fan and media attention. Nobody knew the names of the camera and editing crews, nobody was interested enough to learn who they were. Why should they? To the fans of *Victorious*, he was as invisible as his camera.

And he wouldn't have it any other way.

Every morning, as close to dawn as possible, the *Victorious* crew arrived by boat on the side of the island where the contestants dwelled in their makeshift camp. There was a shorter, more direct route through the jungle forest, but it was never used by the crew. That might've tipped off the contestants, who weren't permitted to know how close they really were to the amenities of civilization in the crew's camp. Plus, lugging all the equipment on foot via jungle pathways was impractical.

Ty eyed the contestants' camp, a familiar sight to him after filming it all this time. It would've been considered a squalid setting if it weren't located on a gorgeous island in the Pacific—and if the inhabitants weren't in a voluntary contest to win a million dollars.

Those factors turned "squalid" into something else entirely, Ty had remarked—innocuously enough, he'd thought—to the show's executive producer, Clark Garrett, who had coldly ordered him to "can the laughter."

So much for small talk with the brass, Ty told his crew later. He hadn't even been trying for laughs.

But though he mocked it, Ty did understand the network obsession with *Victorious*. After all, when the number of reality shows had proliferated on all the networks a few years ago, the TV-viewing public had tired of them. Audiences began tuning out in droves and ratings plummeted. Companies would no longer pay the exorbitant rates charged for advertising spots throughout the shows.

No advertising revenue meant no profits, the networks' worst nightmare.

Eventually all the shows were canceled, no new ones were developed and the reality-TV craze was officially pronounced dead.

And then, one of the networks decided to resurrect the concept to schedule in the moribund Saturday-evening time slot. Ty knew that television executives assumed that nobody under ninety was actually at home watching network TV on Saturday night, but airing a test pattern was not acceptable, and even the worst sitcoms or dramas were expensive to produce.

So the new show *Victorious* was born. With a few variations, it was still pretty much a shameless clone of the original reality game show that had started it all. And with no star salaries and writers to pay, even the million-dollar prize money was deemed cheap.

Just right for Saturday-night television.

When Ty landed the job, he'd learned that *Victorious* was to be filmed and edited on location, a deserted island in the Pacific, for sixty-three days. Within the same week of shooting, the footage would be edited into a one-hour episode and then broadcast.

"It's 'truly live television,'" proclaimed executive producer Clark Garrett. "Or fairly close to it." Clark hyped the fact that nobody, not even he, would know who won the million-dollar prize until just before the last show aired.

The sixteen participants, divided into two tribes of eight each and flown to the gorgeous tropical island, were all telegenic in their own way, some more than others. Currently, the cast was trimmed to six, after combining the survivors of the original two tribes into a single one.

Ty and the crew assembled their equipment while waiting for the remaining six contestants to straggle out of the mosquito netting and bamboo posts that served as their sleeping quarters. The contestants called it a tent, though Ty thought it looked more like a shredded parachute that had fallen out of the sky and landed on some random sticks of bamboo. He wisely declined to share this observation with the ever-testy Clark Garrett.

As usual, the crew filmed each contestant emerging from the tent, from earliest risers to sleep-in slackers. The order never varied from day to day. The Cullen twins, Shannen and Lauren, were always the first up and out; Jed was always last. Rico, Cortnee and Konrad, in varying order, appeared sometime after the twins and well before Jed.

The six had all been members of the same tribe initially and formed an unlikely but ultimately unbeatable alliance, always voting as a block and never against each other. They'd survived while everybody else was voted off the island.

With the crew's camp Internet access, satellite dish and daily newspaper drops, Ty knew that the Final Six had become subjects for water-cooler discussions in offices on Monday morning all over the country. Watching *Victorious* before going out on Saturday night had become the newest fad in the coveted eighteen-to-thirty-four demographic age group, and the network execs were giddy with joy.

He was also aware that the contestants had no clue that ratings for the show had skyrocketed, and the media buzz about each participant was in high gear. The six were isolated from any contact with the outside world and unaware of their new fame.

Ty wondered how much the exposure would affect them, how they would change when back in the real world. He'd wager that it would and they would. He'd learned that lesson only too well from the glare of the Howes' media coverage.

He pointed his camera at the twin sisters splashing water on their faces in their morning wake-up ritual at the small freshwater spring, an idyllic spot where the beach blended into the jungle opening. He was well aware that the twins had found the spring themselves while exploring the island in the first few hours after their arrival, making them heroines to their tribe. Fans speculated that the game-winning alliance had begun then and there.

"Who's your favorite contestant?" asked Heidi, the young production assistant, who stood beside Ty as he was filming.

She asked that question every day or two, more to alleviate boredom than from any real desire to know, Ty suspected. Still, he wasn't about to give out that information, not to anyone.

He said what he always said, remaining scrupulously neutral. "They all have their good and bad days."

"Well, my favorites are the twins," said Heidi.

"You and a lot of others." Ty remained noncommittal, as usual.

"Identical twins are a novelty on any show," Heidi pointed out, not for the first time. "And according to *TV Guide Online,* these two are *incredibly* identical. Wow, like, how true! We've been filming them for weeks, and nobody here can tell them apart yet. Naturally, the viewers can't, either."

"Naturally," Ty echoed dryly. It was true, though. Twenty-six-year-old Shannen and Lauren Cullen were virtual mirror images.

"What would it be like to look like that? *And* be in duplicate?" Heidi wondered aloud. "They're so pretty," she added matter-of-factly.

What could he do but nod in agreement?

The Cullen twins were pretty. Very pretty. Striking brunettes with thick, shoulder-length dark hair and big blue eyes fringed with black lashes. With their youth, their fair skin and delicate bone structure, they had no need for makeup. An application of sunscreen, a quick swipe of the brush through their hair, and the twins were ready to face the day—and the camera crew and the challenges to stay on the island till the end and win the million-dollar prize.

That only one person could win, and that perhaps one twin might have to vote against the other, was an observation made frequently by the program's host, Bobby Dixon, often referred to as Slick Bobby by the *Victorious* contestants. To his face. But while on camera, Bobby's deep-dimpled smile never faltered.

Ty filmed the next contestant who crawled out from the tent. It was Cortnee, a self-described "aspiring superstar," who was using her stint on *Victorious* as a showcase for her singing and dancing talents. At twenty-two, blond, curvaceous Cortnee was the youngest contestant on the island.

Next came Rico, charismatic, energetic and twenty-five, who also aspired to stardom. His singing and dancing talents equaled Cortnee's. Often the pair entertained their fellow contestants with impromptu duets and dances.

And for those viewers not enthralled by the performances, there was always Shannen's stare of irritable impatience to look forward to. Ty always turned his camera on her during a spontaneous Rico and Cortnee number and lingered on her scowl.

Her exasperated mutter, "On no, not again!" was on its way to becoming as much of a highlight as the act itself.

The "evil twin," "the cranky one," Shannen was dubbed on the Web sites devoted to dissecting each episode and each person on the island. Lauren was the "good twin," the nice, sweet one. Not that anybody could tell the sisters apart physically. But "Spitfire Shannen" distinguished herself from "Lady Lauren" every time she raised one dark brow, enhancing the power of her steely signature glare.

Then there was muscular, handsome Jed, twenty-eight, who boasted a résumé including adventure guide, which he proved by excelling in every physical challenge. He spent most of the time in a minimum of clothing, keeping his sculpted body well oiled with the bottle of emollient he'd chosen to bring as his luxury item.

And finally there was Konrad, the oldest of the group at thirty, a former convicted felon who'd arrived on the island sporting a shaved head with a tattoo of a snarling wolf spanning his back. He had other tattoos, on his chest and both arms, all of vicious animals or birds of prey. Konrad spoke in a growl and had never smiled once during the episodes filmed.

His first remark in the first episode—"I paid my debt to society and I want to go straight. If I win, I will. But if I lose, well, I learned plenty in prison to become a world-class burglar. Good skills to fall back on"—had been widely quoted on the Internet discussion boards, drawing both disapproving and admiring responses.

Ty withheld judgment, wondering if Konrad was actually serious. Was the burglary remark a threat? Or was he merely playing to the audience like Rico and Cortnee, though in a very different way?

Everyone, including the crew, agreed that these contestants shared a definite chemistry. Viewers speculated endlessly about the off-camera goings-on based on the contestants' on-screen behavior.

Had the twins and/or Cortnee slept with Rico and/or Jed? Had Rico and Jed slept together? It was unanimously concluded that no one would get physical with Konrad.

The crew did their own speculating about such matters, Ty sometimes joining in, striving for an air of nonchalance about the whole thing. His name was enough of a secret to keep around here; there was certainly no need to introduce his other secret, which would be even more significant to the *Victorious* crew.

However, there was one person right here on the island who knew both his secrets.

One word while the cameras rolled—while *he* made them roll!—and the horrible media circus that had propelled the Howes into the worst kind of fame could start all over again.

And one word about his previous relationship with Shannen Cullen could probably get him fired.

But Shannen didn't give him away, and Ty began to think that perhaps she didn't remember him, after all. It was a definite blow, particularly since he'd admitted to himself long ago that he would never forget her. Seeing her again after long years apart only affirmed her visceral imprint on him.

It would be a fitting irony that she'd forgotten him, a Howe's just desserts, Ty decided wryly. So he came to accept that when Shannen Cullen glared at him, raising that dark eyebrow of hers as he pointed the camera at her, it was nothing personal. Shannen glared at everybody behind

the cameras. He wouldn't delude himself that she was singling out him for any special animosity.

But he couldn't help singling *her* out. He couldn't keep
his eyes off her—nor could he keep his camera away from
her for long. Luckily, she had a twin sister, which seemed
to make the film time equal, since nobody else could tell
the twins apart.

Tynan had no trouble differentiating Shannen from Lauren. He knew ''his'' twin instantly, at first glance every
time, whether the sisters were alone or together. There was
no way to explain how, he just *knew*.

Despite his determination to be different from the other
members of his family, it seemed that he was as foolish
and dysfunctional as any other Howe, Ty mocked himself.
How like a Howe to develop an unhealthy fascination with
the very person who could wreck the normal, productive
life he'd worked so hard to create.

But his unhealthy fascination with Shannen was not new.
Worse, it was as urgent and powerful as it had been nine
years ago. More so because now she had become the
woman he'd thought she was, back when she had been just
a girl.

He'd wanted her then, but he wanted her more now.

And he couldn't have her. Not then and not now.

Being chief cameraman had its perks, one of them being
his own private tent in the camp. It was not as large as
Bobby Dixon's or Clark Garrett's abodes, of course, but
definitely more spacious than the tents that the assistant
camera crew had to share. The editing team were likewise
housed according to their positions, while the production
assistants shared the most cramped quarters, befitting their
slavelike status.

The crew had knocked off filming early at eight o'clock
tonight, on Clark's orders. By the time Ty returned to his

tent from the dinner provided by the catering service, it was almost dark.

The sunsets in the region were nothing less than spectacular, and during his first days on the island, Ty had been dazzled as he filmed them. Now he scarcely glanced at the colorful sky as he called good-night to Reggie and the others.

He'd passed on the invitation to play cards, to monitor the Internet, to watch TV from the satellite dish and all other group activities. He wanted to get to bed early; he was tired and hadn't been sleeping well.

Too many nights in a row he'd awakened from particularly vivid dreams of Shannen Cullen, dreams that left him frustrated when, technically, he should've been replete. It was humiliating to be betrayed by his own body this way. He was thirty-four, not seventeen!

Spending hour after hour filming Shannen, watching her every move yet being unable to approach her, was taking its toll on him, Ty decided grimly. He was on his way to becoming unhinged....

He spied the note on his pillow as soon as he entered his tent. It was written on stationery with the network logo imprinted on the top, and he reached for it, more than a little bemused.

Nobody left notes for others in their tents; that was just too summer camp. Which undoubtedly explained its origins. It had to be one of the crew's practical jokes, probably hatched by the production assistants, Ty surmised. Despite being run ragged by everyone involved with the production, those kids never seemed to run out of energy. And they were into playing pranks, though until now, the gags were directed at one another. Now it seemed that they'd moved up to the senior ranks, Ty thought wryly.

His eyes widened at the sight of the unmistakably feminine handwriting. Then he read the note....

It was a joke—it had to be!

He thought of his brief conversation with Heidi today about the Cullen twins. Was that the beginning of the setup? How else to explain this note, signed "Shannen," ordering him to meet her tonight at a very specific location?

Ty couldn't even summon a laugh at the jest. To him, it wasn't funny—it was appalling! Had he given himself away? He thought he'd remained impeccably indifferent to Shannen Cullen while filming her, but had some of the staffers seen through him?

He wouldn't go, of course. The best way to react to such a practical joke was to blow it off.

But what if this note actually *was* from Shannen?

The renegade thought leaped into his head and took hold. He tried to dislodge it with logic. How would Shannen get hold of network stationery, for starters?

Perversely, he was able to answer what should have been an unanswerable question. If she'd found her way to the crew's camp—to his tent!—swiping a piece of official stationery would be a piece of cake.

Should he go to the trysting place tonight?

Of course he shouldn't!

Ty spent the next two hours debating what to do and finally decided that he *would* go. And he decided, as well, that when he saw one of the PAs—Heidi or Debbie or Adam or Kevin—he would laugh heartily and then accuse whomever, girl or guy, of having a fervid crush on Jed. Or Rico or Cortnee. Or even Konrad. Then he would write the PA in question notes every night, allegedly from the "crush." He'd let Reggie and the rest of the camera crew in on the joke.

He would make the lives of those bratty production assistants a living hell for daring to notice his attraction—okay, maybe it was closer to an obsession!—with Shannen Cullen.

"So you actually showed up."

It sounded more like an accusation than an observation.

Shannen was glowering at him. The brilliance of the full moon illuminated her face as clearly as studio lighting. The air was thick with the exotic scents of tropical plants and the piercing calls of nocturnal birds.

Ty wondered if his eyes were popping out of his skull. Was it possible for his heartbeat to skyrocket this high and still sustain life?

But Shannen was the epitome of cool, just as she was during the days of filming. No eyes popping or thundering pulses for *her* at the sight of *him,* so Ty carefully maintained an imperturbable facade of his own.

He shrugged. ''I have to admit I was surprised to find your note requesting me to meet you here,'' he replied, his voice equally casual. ''I'm curious. How did you manage to—''

''I managed to, okay?'' Her blue eyes flashed.

''Okay.'' He waited for her to tell him the reason why she'd demanded this meeting.

And though he had tactfully rephrased it as a ''request,'' it was not. It had been a demand, and they both knew it. The demanding tenor of the note was one of the main reasons he'd decided it had to be a practical joke. Shannen Cullen wouldn't order him to meet her.

And yet it appeared that she'd done exactly that, because here she was.

Here they both were.

Shannen said nothing.

Silence stretched between them. It occurred to Ty that she was waiting for him to speak first. And that no matter how long the silence lasted, she was prepared to outwait him.

Ty heaved a sigh. ''You're strategizing, aren't you? Can you stop playing the infernal game for just a few minutes and—''

''Play the game or be played. Isn't that how it goes?''

she challenged, her tone mocking. "Well, since you see me as a master strategist, can you guess what my alleged strategy is?"

"Time to check your ego, honey. I didn't say I saw you as a master strategist."

She shot him a fierce look of contempt, a look that would've sent a more cautious man running. But Ty had never been particularly cautious, so he stayed where he was.

"Definitely not a master," he reiterated. He was pleased he'd gotten under her skin, at least a little. "Your ploy is right out of Strategy 101, the course for beginners. You believe you'll gain an advantage if I have to ask why you *demanded* this meeting."

This time he not only used the correct word, he emphasized it. Just a bit of his own simple strategy. Plus, he was certain it would annoy her.

It did. "Don't call me honey! And it was a request, not a demand. A polite request," she added loftily.

"Not going to concede an inch, hmm?" He laughed, a peculiar lightheartedness flooding him. "Just like old times."

"Are you trying to be ironic?" She fairly spat the words at him. "If you are, it's not working. Oh, just forget it! Forget that I wrote that stupid note and—"

"Suppose I willingly and knowingly succumb to your masterful strategy instead. Why did you *politely request* to meet me here tonight?"

Shannen took a deep breath and averted her eyes. "I...I want you to stop following me around," she said sternly.

It was a jaw-dropping moment that left him totally nonplussed. "You're joking," he murmured uncertainly, for neither her tone nor her expression held even the hint of a joke. "Or maybe *you're* trying to be ironic? Given the circumstances of—"

"You know exactly what I mean," she snapped.

"I certainly don't. And let's not forget that *you* demanded to see *me* tonight. It'll be interesting to hear you rationalize how I followed you when you set up this meeting yourself."

Her eyes narrowed into slits. She was furious.

He grinned, unable to resist baiting her further. "Would it be gameworthy of me to point out that I have a job to do, and you have a role, so to speak, which makes—"

"This goes beyond any job or any role, and you know it," she said. "I've seen the way you watch me. You're always staring at me, always filming me. Don't bother to deny it."

"Ah, in addition to your many other charms, you're also paranoid…little girl," he added pointedly.

She picked up his point instantly. "I am not a little girl, you…you—"

"Condescending, self-righteous jerk?" he suggested. "Oh yes, I remember that, Shannen. I remember everything. But I wasn't sure that you did, not until I got your note tonight."

He didn't bother to add how he'd decided the note was bogus. He was too elated that it was real.

"You thought I didn't remember you?" For a moment Shannen looked genuinely surprised, but she quickly resumed hostilities. "Well, I do—and it's obvious that the description still fits you. You're still condescending, you're still self-righteous and you're still a jerk!"

"How would you know? This is the first time we've spoken since—"

"A tiger never changes its stripes," she said. "Or is it a leopard who doesn't change its spots? Oh, who cares! I know I can—"

She abruptly stopped speaking when he advanced toward her.

"You can what?" He stood directly in front of her, towering over her.

The aroma of saltwater and sunscreen, mixed with an alluring scent all her own, filled his nostrils. "You can what?" he repeated huskily.

She swallowed. "I...I forget."

"How about this, then? You can prove you're not a little girl anymore?"

Her eyes widened as he slowly lowered his head toward her. His hands were at his sides and he made no attempt to hold her in place or restrain her in any way.

She could easily have stepped aside or pushed him away; she could've ordered him to go back from her or made a threat that would have sent him on his way.

But she did none of those things. Slowly Shannen raised her arms to encircle his neck. Their gazes locked and held for a long moment. He watched her eyelids flutter shut as he touched his mouth to hers.

What began as a light, tentative caress of his lips against hers quickly turned into something else entirely. There was nothing light or tentative about the hot, hungry coupling of their mouths.

Ty murmured something unintelligible as her lips parted to welcome his tongue inside.

Shannen pressed closer, twisting restlessly against him, opening her mouth wider in sensual invitation. He accepted, deepening the kiss, thrusting his knee between her thighs and molding her to him, his hands smoothing over her, possessively, eagerly learning every curve.

The kiss went on and on, desire building, passion burning. Ty slowly lowered her to the ground, pulling her on top of him. His fingers nimbly opened the clasp of her halter top, freeing her breasts. His hand cupped one soft milky-white breast, and he groaned with pleasure.

A split second later, he was lying on the sand alone. Shannen had pulled away from him and jumped to her feet with disorienting speed.

"No!" she exclaimed, fumbling to close the clasp he had

so effortlessly undone. Her dexterity didn't equal his and she gave up, holding the halter together with one hand.

Ty rose slowly, almost painfully, to his feet. "Let me help you with that."

She backed away from him as if he were radioactive. "Go away! I...I told you to keep away from me."

"Yes, you did." His lips twisted into a wry smile. "But your message was—hmm, how can I put this tactfully?—mixed."

She flushed scarlet, the bright moonlight highlighting her color. "You're a snake!"

"I've been called worse." He ran his hand through his dark hair. "Anything else?"

"I don't know what you're doing here or who you're pretending to be or why, but I don't trust you!"

"Thanks." Ty chuckled softly. "And let me return the compliment. I don't trust you, either."

Shannen turned and stomped away from him, still clutching her top with one hand, using her other hand to smack away the hanging vines and lush foliage that dared get in her way.

Ty stood watching until she disappeared from view.

Two

"Do you think we'll get mail-in-the-tree today? Or a visit from Slick Bobby with some kind of instructions?" Cortnee asked during her rigorous aerobic workout, which she performed daily on the beach. Today she wore her tiniest bikini, the neon-pink one. "We haven't had a victory contest or a food contest this week."

Konrad, Rico and Jed gathered on the beach in various positions of repose, watching Cortnee. The twins were there, too, Lauren braiding her hair into a thick plait, Shannen tying strings to three makeshift bamboo fishing poles.

"I checked the tree for mail earlier and there wasn't anything," Shannen reported. "Why don't one of you guys go check it now?"

"Later," said Jed.

"And we're almost out of bait," continued Shannen. "Somebody should go to that place farther down the beach and see if more clams have washed up. That's the best bait on the island."

"Later," murmured Rico.

"We can check for tree mail and then swing down for clams after we fish, Shannen," Lauren suggested.

"I just thought maybe someone else would like a chance to do the daily errands around here," murmured Shannen, adding tersely, "for a change."

"Remember how those idiots in the other tribe ate some bad raw clams instead of cutting them up for bait?" Konrad sniggered. "Man, were they sick! When they tried to hang on to the rope in that tug-of-war between the tribes, they fell flat on their faces." Clearly, it was a fond memory for him.

"Our tribe won every single contest, forcing the other tribe to keep voting off their own till they were all gone," observed Jed. He began idly doodling in the sand with a stick.

"We won all the contests, so our tribe was able to stay intact a long time, and it's mainly thanks to you, Jed," Lauren said, her voice filled with admiration.

Jed nodded his head. "True."

"Partially true," corrected Shannen. "You forgot to add that you couldn't have done it alone, Jed. I didn't hear you say that all of us did our part to win, either. Did you forget that we're a team?"

"Jed isn't a team player—he doesn't want to share credit for anything," Cortnee called between deep breaths. "He really believes he does *everything* better than anybody else."

Jed opened his mouth to speak, but Rico beat him to it by sighing heavily, gaining the attention of the cameramen. "I just want to say that I don't miss the other tribe because I barely knew them, but I do miss Keri and Lucy from our tribe." Rico sighed again. "I really bonded with them. They were probably some of the best friends I ever had in my life."

"You voted them off the island without blinking an eye, Rico," Shannen pointed out.

"Untrue!" protested Rico. "Maybe it looked that way because I hid my pain so well, but I've been torturing myself for getting involved in this unholy alliance with you guys. You made me turn against my friends!"

His face a portrait of agony, Rico stared soulfully into the camera that had been turned on him the moment he began to speak. He pouted when the camera abruptly shifted to Shannen, who was now baiting the hooks, frowning in concentration.

"Cut to the evil twin. Nice move, Ty," junior cameraman Reggie Ellis whispered to Ty, who was filming Shannen. "Makes for good TV. She looks distinctly unmoved by Rico's brooding torment. Like she's remembering how Rico was the first to suggest that they 'vote off those schemers Keri and Lucy because they're allied against us.' The viewers will remember, that's for sure."

"Rico wants to show the talent agents who'll be watching that he has range," Ty said dryly. "That he's not just a song-and-dance man."

"Yeah, he's good at brooding and backstabbing," Reggie observed. "The kid does have that slightly sleazy manner about him, too. A handy survival trait in showbiz."

"I can see Rico winning an Oscar someday. Unless he decides to run for political office instead," murmured Ty. "He'd do well in that arena, too."

Having completed her task of baiting the hooks, Shannen looked up and saw Ty filming her. She shot him a withering glare before looking away.

"Looks like she'd enjoy baiting those hooks with pieces of you, Ty." Reggie guffawed. "Y'know, for somebody who volunteered to be on this show, she sure hates having the camera on her. I think I'm starting to be able to tell which twin is which, just from that. Lauren doesn't pay any attention to the camera, but Shannen looks as if she'd like to shove it down your throat.''

''You noticed that, too?'' Ty was casual.

Reggie nodded. ''We're not the only ones to wonder. I logged onto the Internet last night, and there's a debate going on as to why the twins auditioned to be on this show in the first place. Especially since Shannen looks eternally ticked off because she's here.''

''Remember their interview tapes? Both twins said they did it as a lark,'' said Ty.

He didn't add that he wondered himself why the Cullen twins had auditioned for the show. The ''for a lark'' reason didn't ring true to him. Nine years ago Shannen's behavior had been quite purposeful. Filming her every day here on the island didn't contradict his impression that she was a person who rarely made an unplanned move.

But there had been nothing calculated about that hot kiss they'd shared last night. It had been as impetuous as it was passionate. Ty tried to tamp down his nascent arousal.

''Maybe Lauren did it as a lark, but Shannen doesn't strike me as the lark type.'' Reggie chuckled. ''If we're talking birds, she's more of a shrike. You know, the one that impales its prey on a stake. Oh, Ty, quick, pan over to Cortnee. She has her back to us and is touching her toes. Every red-blooded male in the audience is gonna love that. And she's wearing that pink thong bikini that almost caused a meltdown on the Internet the first time she put it on.''

''You can have the pleasure of filming her, Reg. I know you're one of Cortnee's top fans. I'll keep my camera on the twins and Konrad. Looks like they're going fishing.''

Each carrying a primitive bamboo fishing pole, Shannen, Lauren and Konrad walked briskly into the ocean. Ty followed close behind, camera whirling.

''Do you think we should go out in the rowboat?'' asked Lauren as the surf broke around their knees. ''We might have better luck catching fish in deeper water.''

"Yeah, but then we'd have the fun of swimming with the sharks when that leaky old tub sinks," growled Konrad. "Remember when those two idiots in the other tribe took the boat out and it went down like a stone with them in it? Had that big dramatic rescue 'cause they couldn't swim. You know Slick Bobby and Clark Garrett woulda rather seen them drown. And now they claim the boat's fixed, but I don't buy it. They're still hoping to get lucky with a fatal accident."

"That's entertainment for those two human piranhas," Shannen pointed out.

"Never mind the boat, then, let's try our luck right here," suggested Lauren, casting her pole. "Oh, don't look now, but we're on camera again. I was sure the whole crew would stay on the beach filming Cortnee. Doesn't she do her jumping jacks after touching her toes? None of the guys want to miss that."

"Gets old when you see the same stuff day after day." Konrad shrugged. "Me, I'd rather hang out with you two, even though I don't know which the hell is which."

"Konrad, how gallant!" Lauren smiled sweetly.

Shannen turned her head to see Ty standing less than a foot behind them. She swung her fishing line at him, clipping him with the clam bait.

"Oops." She snickered. "So sorry."

"You're only sorry that your aim was off." Ty turned off the camera. "You meant to smack me in the face with the clam guts. But you missed, Shannen," he added, saying her name with alacrity.

"You're sure I'm Shannen?" She looked ready to whip the pole at him again. "How do you know I'm not Lauren?"

"Could be, you know," Lauren chimed in. "We're dressed exactly alike. Denim cutoffs, red bandanna triangle tops. The only difference is that one of us has a braid and the other has a ponytail. Can you be sure who styled her hair which way?''

''You two play that twin stuff for all it's worth,'' said Konrad, with respect. ''No wonder. Two people looking exactly the same…talk about messing with minds! If I had a twin in the lineup with me, nobody could ID me. Because it might be my twin, y'know? I could've beat the rap every time.''

''We'll keep that in mind if we decide to go in for a life of crime, Konrad,'' said Shannen.

''I don't have a problem telling them apart.'' Ty moved closer to Shannen. ''This is Shannen. Unquestionably.''

When she took a step backward, he advanced, knowing she would force herself not to retreat again. She would view that as a tactical error.

He was right. She stayed put.

''Remember the rules? The crew isn't supposed to interact with us in any way.'' Shannen's fingers clenched the pole tightly, and she stayed as still as she could, despite the unsteadying waves rising and breaking around her. ''You're supposed to be invisible. So shut up and film, Tynan.''

''Who's to know I'm not? From on shore, it looks like I'm filming the three of you out here.''

''How do you know his name, Shan?'' Lauren was puzzled. ''We weren't introduced to any of the crew. Clark and Bobby said to think of them as part of the camera equipment and forget they're human.''

''Which isn't hard to do, in his case,'' Shannen sneered.

''You dodged the question, babe.'' Konrad studied her curiously. ''How come you know his name?''

''Maybe she made a good guess. Am I right, Shannen?'' Ty's bland tone contrasted sharply to his baiting smile.

''As a matter of fact, you are. I read a book about names, and Tynan means 'condescending, self-righteous jerk,' so I immediately guessed he must be a Tynan." Shannen met and held his gaze. "An obvious fit."

"If Cortnee was out here, she'd say, 'What did the book say that Cortnee means?'" Konrad laughed.

It was a startling moment. Shannen recovered first.

"The first time Konrad laughs, and you aren't filming, Tynan," she scolded. "You're not doing your job. I ought to tell Slick Bobby next time he oozes by so he can pass it on to Clark. Then you'll get fired."

"But you won't tell, will you, Shannen?" Ty leaned down to wash off the bits of clam that clung to his bare shoulder. Like the other cameramen, he rarely wore a shirt during the long days of filming in the sun. He was bronzed and muscular.

Shannen quickly looked away from him, staring instead into the sparkling clear water.

"How do you know my sister won't tell on you?" demanded Lauren, her eyes darting from Shannen to Ty and back again.

"Because I read the same name book that she did, and Shannen means 'not a snitch,'" said Ty.

"A bitch but not a snitch," amended Konrad.

Lauren stamped her foot. "My sister is not a bitch! You should apologize to Shannen right now, Konrad."

"He doesn't have to, I've been called worse names than that." Shannen stole a glance at Ty. When she found him staring at her, she looked away again. "It doesn't bother me."

"I'm sure whoever called you…worse names, regrets doing so, Shannen," Tynan said quietly.

"I'm sure I don't care, Tynan," she retorted. "Sticks and stones and all that."

"Y'know, that's just crap," Konrad said vehemently. "Some of the names I got called as a kid made me a helluva lot madder than getting whacked with any stick. And in the joint, you better watch your mouth—you get what

I'm saying? You diss somebody there and you're dead meat. It's worse than punching him out.''

"That's an interesting point." Ty raised his camera. "Would you say that again when I turn the camera back on?''

"Sure." Konrad looked pleased. "Uh, should she say the bit about sticks and stones before I say it?''

"Yeah, that's good." Ty nodded. "Shannen?''

"I'm not saying anything," Shannen said crossly. "You aren't directing a movie, and we're not supposed to rehearse our lines. Get out of here, Tynan. Go back and film Cortnee.''

"Hey, I made an interesting point," argued Konrad. "It should be on TV.''

"I'll give you a lead-in, Konrad," Lauren volunteered. "Okay, Tynan, 'Camera, action, take one,' or however that drill goes." She tilted her head, her expression suddenly wistful. "Shannen, remember how the kids at school used to call us freaky clones? And Gramma told us to say, 'Sticks and stones may break our bones but names will never hurt us.'''

"Who called you freaky clones?" demanded Konrad. "Just tell me who and when I get back *I'll* break every bone in *their*—''

"Nobody ever called us that." Shannen heaved an exasperated sigh. "It was just Lauren's cue for you to say your—oh, turn off that camera, Ty. This is ridiculous.''

Ty turned off the camera. "Makes you really respect directors, doesn't it? Imagine doing take after take after take of the same botched scene.''

"Acting is harder than I thought," admitted Konrad. "Care to try it over again?''

"No!" Tynan and the twins chorused.

The four of them looked at each other and laughed. They immediately lapsed into silence, nonplussed by the unexpected moment of camaraderie.

"I got a fish!" Lauren suddenly shrieked, hanging on to her bamboo pole, which was waving and twitching. "I bet it's big, it's really strong! Help!"

Tynan turned on his camera to film Lauren clutching her fishing pole as it swayed precariously, back and forth and around. Konrad reached over and took hold of the string, swinging it out of the water. The fish on the primitively fashioned hook went flying into the air.

"Get it! Get it!" cried Lauren.

Konrad did, catching the impressive-size fish with his bare hands.

"That was so quick!" marveled Shannen. "Like watching Gramma's cat reach up and nab the bird who'd made the fatal mistake of flying onto the porch while he was napping there."

"Except we can eat the fish," said Lauren. "That bird incident—yuck, it was so gross!"

Ty's lips quirked. He caught Shannen's eye and found her looking at him. Both immediately turned their attention back to Konrad and the fish.

"I think I'll turn off the camera until that fish is officially pronounced dead," said Ty.

"Feeling queasy, Ty?" taunted Shannen. "You didn't seem to have any qualms filming us drinking snake blood in that over-the-top victory contest a couple weeks ago."

"The snake blood scene was sexy in a vampire-ish sort of way, to quote a TV critic," said Ty. "But nobody is going to find strangling a fish sexy in any sort of way."

"That's disgusting!" scolded Shannen.

Ty wondered if she was referring to him, snake blood or fish strangulation.

"The fish is dead," announced Konrad.

Ty resumed filming.

"This fish would make a decent-size meal for two people, maybe even three, but we'll only have a few mouthfuls each if we split it six ways," said Konrad. "So let's not."

"It's only fair to share it with everybody," insisted Lauren.

"We could outvote her." Konrad turned to Shannen. "Two against one not to share."

"My stomach wants to go along with you, but my better instincts tell me that Lauren is right." Shannen sighed.

"Better instincts? More like idiotic instincts," Konrad muttered, then added a few unintelligible growls as they trooped back to shore.

Cortnee was so delighted to see the fish, she squealed with joy and hugged Konrad and the twins in turn.

Rico and Jed tried to look happy but weren't altogether convincing.

"Their smiles are so fake, I'm surprised their faces haven't cracked," observed Shannen to no one in particular. "They want to be the heroes, but you can't catch anything, lounging around on the beach all day."

"Told you it was stupid to share," Konrad needled her.

Ty noticed that Reggie had moved closer to film the group, and he turned off his own camera. "Shannen." His voice was lower than a whisper, but Shannen heard.

"Don't talk to me," she warned, her voice even quieter than his.

It was a warning Ty didn't heed. "Meet me tonight. Same time and place as last night."

"No!" She looked alarmed. "I can't! I…I—" She was truly rattled.

"Be there," said Ty, and moved away from her.

"Shannen, what's wrong?" Lauren called out to her.

Shannen looked up to see Reggie, a few feet away, filming her.

Lauren was staring at her, confused. "You look—you don't look happy, Shan."

"Maybe she's jealous because she wasn't the one to catch the fish," mocked Jed.

"Maybe I'm not happy because I expect you'll try to

grab yourself some glory and insist on cooking the fish yourself," Shannen countered. "Thereby rendering it inedible."

Jed took instant umbrage. "I'm a damn good cook. I even contributed a recipe that I invented myself to the *Living off the Land* cookbook."

"What was it, how to barbecue roadkill?" Konrad snickered. "Step one, you pick it off the side of the road. Step two—"

"It was how to make elk stew," Jed inserted disdainfully. "And—"

"Whatever," snapped Cortnee. "Just don't get anywhere near this fish!"

"He's only had a few cooking…mishaps here on the island." Lauren tried to make peace.

"You mean disasters, not mishaps," corrected Rico.

"I've never cooked a bad meal," Jed said huffily. "You're all just a bunch of picky eaters."

"Jed's already proved that he doesn't know the difference between cooking something or cremating it," Shannen said flatly. "I vote that he *not* cook the fish."

"I'm with you, twin," said Rico.

"Me, too," said Konrad.

"You've got my vote," said Cortnee.

"Are we seeing cracks in what has previously been a staunch and solid alliance?" Bobby Dixon asked in his smiling, smooth soliloquy, filmed a mile down the beach.

A light breeze ruffled his thick hair and he smoothed it down with his hand, dimpling deeply.

"Tonight, after the victory contest, these six survivors, who have stuck together from the very beginning, will have to vote out one of their own." His voice took on a note of urgency and suspense. "What shifts of allegiance will occur to form new alliances as we count down to five and then to the Final Four? Who has what it takes to be *Victorious?*''

Later the six contestants gathered around the fire, eating the fish cooked by the twins.

"That was great," Rico said expansively, patting his washboard stomach. "If the food is as good at that diner your family owns, I'm heading there as soon as we're off this island."

"Shannen and I have been short-order cooks since we were in junior high," said Lauren. "Of course, it's much easier at home, because we don't have to catch the food ourselves."

"Well, no matter what you hear, the food in prison isn't bad," Konrad interjected. "And you get more of it than one lousy fish split six ways."

"I'm still hungry," wailed Cortnee. "Having only a couple bites of fish and a blob of wretched rice is like being on a starvation diet."

"I cooked the rice and it wasn't wretched, it was fine," snarled Jed.

"It really wasn't wretched at all," Lauren hastily agreed.

"Uh-oh, look what's headed our way." Shannen was the first to spy Bobby Dixon strolling down the beach toward them, wearing his immaculately pressed khaki slacks and matching safari shirt.

"He looks so neat and clean all the time, I can't stand it." Cortnee groaned. "It's been how long since we had a hot shower? And washing your hair in the ocean is really bad. There's a reason why saltwater shampoo was never invented."

"Wouldn't it be thrilling to see Slick Bobby look less...dapper?" Shannen flashed a naughty smile. "It might even take my mind off being hungry out here all the time."

"Yeah, but it'll never happen." Rico heaved a disgruntled sigh. "We'll stay hungry as long as we're on the island, and Bobby will stay clean. You just know he has his clothes cleaned and pressed every day over in the crew's camp. And somehow he never sweats, no matter how hot it is."

"Makes you wonder if the guy's human," murmured Shannen. "I've had my doubts. Those dimples of his look like computer animation."

"I bet Slick B would sweat if we poured fish guts over him," said Konrad, staring moodily into the bean can holding the fish remains. They'd saved the can from their first days on the island, to use as a container.

"Anybody want to try it and see?" Rico asked eagerly. "Cortnee? Twins?"

Shannen laughed. "You're evil, Rico."

"Hello, all." Bobby joined them, dimpling at the camera. "No mail-in-the-tree today. I brought the contest requirements to you in person."

"Watch out, Bobby. They've hatched this juvenile plan to drench you in fish guts," Jed called out.

Konrad scowled. "Anybody know what that stoolie is talking about?"

The others shrugged and shook their heads.

"I do know that Jed is a rat." Cortnee sniffed. "And if he didn't win every contest and get himself immunity, I'd gladly vote him off."

"You can dream, but it's never going to happen, babycakes." Jed positioned himself so his sculpted body had full camera advantage. "And keep in mind that we're no longer a team anymore. Now it's everyone for himself—or herself, as the case may be."

"Jed is right," agreed Bobby. "It's everyone for him- or herself, and the contest today is a rowboat race. All six of you will take turns rowing out to the crew's boat and back."

He pointed to the large boat anchored about a hundred

yards out in the sea. "The one with the fastest time, of course, wins immunity in the council vote tonight."

"Have I ever mentioned that I crewed in college?" Jed began his warmup exercises. "And kayaked down the Colorado River when the white water was at its highest and fastest?"

"Kayaks are for sissies," scoffed Shannen. "Lauren and I rode the white water at its highest and fastest using rubber duck floatees."

Shannen glanced up to see Tynan and Reggie chuckling behind their cameras. She pretended not to notice them, turning her attention to Rico and Cortnee, who were also laughing at her joke. But when she looked over at her sister, Lauren wasn't even smiling.

"Are you okay, Lauren?" asked Shannen, concerned. Lauren looked so…cross? Shannen almost did a double take. Was Lauren angry about something? But what?

"Sure." Lauren smiled slightly, shrugging. "I'm fine, Shannen."

"Hey, Jed, my man, since you're so sure you're going to win, would you mind letting us five losers go before you?" Konrad asked with unusual servility. "You know, to build up the suspense and all?"

"I don't mind going last," said Jed. "Although I can't guarantee suspense, because the outcome will never be in doubt. I'm going to win."

"Yeah?" With mercurial speed, Konrad's expression turned to disgust, and he suddenly picked up the can of fish guts and tossed it at Bobby.

But Bobby was on the alert, thanks to Jed, and deftly jumped aside. "That was uncalled for, Konrad!" Bobby was peeved. His clothes, however, remained pristine, as if he'd just picked them up from the dry cleaner's. "You could be disciplined for—"

"Disciplined for a little food-fight fun?" Shannen cut in.

"Where's your sense of humor, Slick B? Anyway, this isn't high school, and you can't 'discipline' anybody."

The crew snickered. Bobby Dixon's off-camera behavior as a prima donna had earned him no friends among them.

"That chick has a righteous attitude," said Heidi. "She doesn't put up with anything from anybody."

"She never has," murmured Ty wryly. "Since she arrived on the island," he was quick to add.

Ty and two others remained on the beach filming, while cameramen Reggie and Paul were stationed on the crew boat, to film the contestants racing to it. Bobby Dixon was also on the boat with a large stopwatch to record the times. The production assistants were scattered in both locations.

Cortnee went first and threw herself down on the sand on her return. "I'm so tired I could faint. That awful rowing took more energy than playing the lead in my senior-class musical." She wiped away tears with the back of her hand.

Rico went next, then Lauren and then Shannen.

"Well, that was hellacious," Shannen groaned, sitting down between Lauren and Rico after her own long row. "My arms feel like they're going to fall off, my hands are getting blistered and I'm exhausted. Not to mention hungrier than ever."

She looked into the camera and met Tynan's eyes. "I'm going to bed right after the council meeting, no matter what."

Slowly Ty turned his head from one side to the other. He mouthed the word "tonight" and watched her jaw drop. Clearly, she was not expecting such obvious interaction with him.

But nobody noticed except her. The others were ignoring the camera and cameraman to watch Konrad push the rowboat into the water.

"I said I'm going straight to bed tonight," Shannen repeated, giving Ty her most forbidding grimace. "Nowhere but my own bed."

"You girls should've done what Konrad is doing," said Jed, who was standing nearby, watching Konrad in the rowboat heading out to sea. "You should've saved your strength and taken your own sweet time, like him. He knows I'm going to win, and since every other score is irrelevant, why wear yourself out?"

He swaggered off toward the water to wait for Konrad to return with the rowboat.

"I hate Jed," Cortnee said fiercely, watching him walk off. "He thinks he's so hot. Did you know he slept with both Keri and Lucy? They each tried to get him to switch his alliance from us to them, and he let them think he would. I wanted to tell you all, but I didn't think the time was right. Till now."

"He slept with both of them?" Lauren gasped. "Cortnee, are you sure?"

"I heard them, I heard everything." Cortnee shuddered. "They were right outside the tent on my side and I'm a light sleeper. I wake up at the slightest noise."

"Do you hear people get up during the night to, um, well—you know?" Shannen was not her usual frank self.

"Uh-huh. I heard you or your sister get up last night to—" Cortnee laughed. "No need to be shy, we're among friends—to use the facilities."

"I can't believe Jed would use Keri and Lucy for sex," said Lauren. "If he did, he would've switched his allegiance from us to them, and he didn't. He was loyal and he stuck with us all this time. You...you must've misinterpreted what you were hearing, Cortnee."

"I know exactly what I heard," insisted Cortnee. "Believe me, I didn't misinterpret a thing."

"The man is slime." Shannen scowled.

"And the reason why Jed didn't switch from us to them is because we five were the stronger choice," Rico pointed out. "Loyalty had nothing to do with it. Too bad we're stuck with him now. He'll keep winning every contest for immunity, and we'll get kicked off, one by one."

"We made our version of a deal with the devil. Now it's time to pay." Shannen looked over at Ty. "Gramma always says, 'If you let the devil into the cart, you'll have to drive him home.' And she wasn't talking about hitchhiking in biblical times."

Ty grinned broadly. Shannen lifted her chin and turned away.

Konrad joined the group after his long, slow turn in the boat race. He looked downright cheerful. "So, tonight we vote out Jed. Everybody cool with that?"

"If only!" Shannen gingerly moved her aching arms and flexed her fingers again. "But Jed'll have the fastest time and win immunity so we *can't* vote against him. We five will have to vote out one of us. Jed is going to be the winner in this game, I think that's screamingly obvious."

"Speaking of screaming." Konrad cocked his head. "Do I hear some?"

"I don't hear anything." Lauren looked around. "Even those screeching monkeys are quiet for a change."

Seconds after she'd uttered that declaration, a scream pierced the tranquil air. All heads turned in the direction of the ocean.

Jed was standing in the boat, yelling at the top of his lungs.

"That was definitely a scream," Shannen said dryly, turning toward Konrad. "A primal one. Is there a scorpion in the boat with Jed or something?"

"It looks like Jed is trying to throw handfuls of water out of the boat." Cortnee looked confused. "Why isn't he rowing?"

"Too bad he doesn't have a bucket," said Konrad. "Lots easier to bail with a bucket than with your hands." He surprised everybody by roaring with laughter.

"The boat's sinking!" exclaimed Rico. "Look, it really is! In another couple minutes, Jed is going to be in the ocean."

"Oh, poor Jed!" cried Lauren.

"Yeah, poor poor Jed." Konrad laughed harder. "Good thing Mister Wilderness Guide is such a strong swimmer, huh?"

"Good thing," agreed Shannen. "Because the rowboat is history. All that's left is an oar. Well, Konrad did say it was a leaky old tub." She shot a quizzical glance at him.

They all stared out at the lone floating oar and at Jed, two far-off blurs in the sea.

"Everybody!" Cortnee cried. "I just thought of something. Since the rowboat sank, Jed won't be able to complete the contest. He won't get immunity. One of us will have the fastest time and one of us will win immunity!"

"It won't be me," predicted Konrad. "I was really slow out there."

"We noticed." Shannen said dryly. "There were times when we couldn't see you at all, you were slouched down so far in the boat. You have an interesting way of rowing, Konrad. And you're good at predictions, too, it seems," she added, raising an eyebrow in his direction.

"Thank you, ma'am." Konrad bowed from the waist.

For a few more minutes they all watched Jed swimming toward the crew's boat as the waves broke over him. There wasn't a trace of the sunken rowboat.

Later, a soaking-wet Jed was returned to shore in the dinghy from the crew boat. He stomped into camp with accusations of sabotage and demanded another chance in another rowboat.

As the cameras continued to roll, he threatened to sue the show and the network and everybody on the island, especially Konrad, if he ultimately won the game.

Bobby Dixon was unmoved. "Sorry, Jed. The rules of the game plainly state that do-overs are never allowed.

There's no proof of any wrongdoing, and the cameras were on the rowboat at all times.''

"On the rowboat, but not on Konrad!" argued Jed. "He got himself out of sight and did something to make it sink, I know he did. He cheated!"

"Not winning is obviously difficult for you, Jed, but you must accept it and move on like everybody else," Bobby said unctuously. "In today's contest, the fastest time was Rico's, and he wins the immunity statue."

Bobby handed Rico the foot-high painted wooden totem pole that looked as if it had been purchased at a roadside souvenir shop.

"This is the first time in the game that anybody but Jed has won that thing," said Shannen. "No one can vote against Rico tonight. Gee, I wonder who everybody will vote off the island?"

Three

———

The full moon had waned only slightly, so the bright path through the tangle of vines and low-hanging branches was as easy to follow as it had been last night. Shannen slowly, carefully made her way, as familiar with it by night as by day.

She had thoroughly explored this island during the long daylight hours, looking for food and anything else that might be useful to their group. She'd easily slipped off alone, when the cameras were fixed on groups of the others.

With Lauren unwittingly serving as a decoy, Shannen's absences went unnoticed. Since the twins weren't always side by side, as long as one of them was in view, who was to say which sister it was? That sort of fungibility sometimes bugged Shannen, but not on this island, not in this game.

Especially since her solo wanderings had provided her with quite a bit of useful information, some of which she didn't share with anybody. Like the undiscovered shortcut to the crew's camp on the other side of the island and the secluded palm grove where she was now headed.

Shannen's heart began to thud heavily.

She'd slipped away from camp tonight, wondering if Cortnee had heard her leave. But there was nothing questionable about someone getting up and heading off "to use the facilities," Shannen reminded herself.

Cortnee hadn't been suspicious last night; plus, she wouldn't know whether it was Lauren or Shannen who'd left on either night.

Certainly the last thing anybody would suspect was that practical, logical, no-nonsense Shannen Cullen was sneaking off to meet the chief cameraman. Not even Lauren, the person who knew her best in the world, would ever fathom that.

But then, there were some things that not even Lauren knew about her twin.

Nine years ago, in the throes of rebellion and intense first love—she'd often wondered how much one had fueled the other—Shannen had stopped sharing every single thought and feeling with Lauren. Her wild passion for Tynan Howe had been the biggest secret she'd ever kept. Deliberately, she hadn't even mentioned his name to her twin.

And though she'd gloried in her secret love, when it was over—after *he'd* ended it—the price she had paid was enduring her heartbreak alone. For the first time in her young life, Shannen hadn't had loyal Lauren to share her pain, thereby halfing it. Another grudge to hold against Tynan Howe, and she'd held fast to it.

Yet now, though supposedly older and wiser, here she was repeating her mistakes—the rebellion against the rules, the secrecy from her sister—and with the same man!

What was happening to that practical, logical and no-nonsense character she'd spent years honing? Why was she sneaking out at midnight, like the recalcitrant teenager she'd once been, to meet Tynan Howe? *Again!*

Nine years ago he had insisted he was too old for her. In her calmer moments back then—and since—she might even have seen his point and agreed. She might've dreamed of a day when she was out of high school, out of her teens, and had reached whatever age Ty deemed "old enough."

But her age wasn't the sole reason cited by Tynan as to why they couldn't be together. It was those other, far more hurtful reasons he had supplied—the reasons she came to believe were his true reasons—that still resonated within her.

Well, she was of legal age now, and thanks to the multiple Howe scandals, Tynan was not quite the "catch" he once had been. Not that she wanted to catch him, Shannen quickly assured herself.

She didn't for many reasons—the current, main one being this game they were playing, on opposite sides of the camera, making Tynan Howe off-limits to her.

It was déjà-vu all over again, as the saying went.

If their clandestine meetings were discovered, she would undoubtedly be kicked out of the game, in full camera view, of course. Clark Garrett and Slick Bobby would want to milk every dramatic possibility.

Lauren would feel so betrayed by her twin's secrecy, both past and present, and the cameras would record her reaction to it all. Shannen flinched at the thought of wounding her sister.

Furthermore, if she were eliminated now, how long would Lauren last without her in the game? From the time they were little, Shannen had felt compelled to protect Lauren, to make sure no one took advantage of her more naive twin.

Would Konrad, Rico and Cortnee gang up on Lauren if her more formidable sister were gone? Being legitimately voted off the island was one thing, but foolishly getting herself kicked out of the game was unacceptable.

Unexpectedly she and Lauren had come this far. Why throw away a possible chance to win?

Though it would be wonderful to win the top prize, just making the final four would be okay, too, Shannen told herself. Being one of the final four meant a cash prize, with each runner-up—the third, the second and, finally, the first—making more in turn.

Were she and Lauren *both* to make the final four, the payoff would be considerable. That was not something to be lightly dismissed.

The Cullen twins hadn't turned over their lives to a prime-time game show for the hell of it. They needed the money—the family was counting on them.

As for the risk Tynan was taking meeting her...

Well, keeping his job because he needed his salary wouldn't be a concern for *him*. Whatever their transgressions, the Howes must still be rich. After all, during the entire time the Howe family had been under the full glare of the media spotlight, one story that had never appeared was their plunge into poverty.

Ty probably wouldn't even lose his job. Wasn't it a universal truth that men rarely paid the same price for breaking the rules that women did? And, of course, Tynan was a Howe, whose family knew a thing or two thousand about rule breaking.

Victorious concerns aside, Tynan Howe was emotionally dangerous to her. Any man who could effortlessly turn back the clock nine years and transform her into her impetuous young-girl self was a must to avoid.

Unfortunately, Shannen couldn't seem to stay focused on all the practical, logical no-nonsense reasons why she should keep away from him. She kept getting distracted by other thoughts.

Like his name. He wasn't even using the name Howe.

She'd realized that the first day they had all arrived on the island. There were no introductions to the crew, but when she'd seen Ty among them—after getting over the initial stunning shock—she had paid close attention. And heard him called Ty Hale.

Hale, not Howe. Scrapping Howe for Hale didn't surprise her nearly as much as the fact that he was working as a television cameraman. After all, the Howe name was no longer a proud symbol of wealth, achievement and privilege. The family had dragged it through so much mud, it had become a stigma.

But Tynan had gone to law school. He'd been a senior law student at West Falls University Law School when they'd met. She knew he'd taken and passed the state bar exam. The names of graduates passing the various state professional examinations always were proudly published in the university newspaper.

Since when did a lawyer work as a cameramen on a network game show? Tynan Hale, attorney at law, made more sense than Tynan Hale, working-stiff cameraman, didn't it?

She wanted to know; she wondered every time she looked at him behind that camera. Which was nearly sixteen hours a day. The omnipresence of the camera crew was annoying enough, but having Ty always there had reawakened feelings she thought—she'd hoped!—had died.

Not so. Never had she been so aware of anyone in her life—except during their last go-round nine long years ago.

So why didn't you ask him all those pertinent questions last night, Shannen? she silently chided herself. Instead, she'd ended up in his arms within minutes, after making that pathetically lame excuse of why she had risked meeting him.

Why *had* she risked meeting him in the first place?

No use pretending she didn't know the answer to that

one. Seeing him every day, all day... Having him so near yet so totally out of reach...

The tension built and burned inside her. Unaccustomed to passivity, she couldn't stop herself from taking action.

Oh, who was she kidding? Shannen exhaled an impatient sigh, unable to talk herself into the convenient self-deception. Taking action and losing control were too very different responses, and she knew which one had prevailed last night.

Memories of last night whirled through her head, making her wince. Tynan had accused her of strategizing by using silence. Thankfully, he hadn't known she'd been struck dumb by the sight of him, by the tantalizing prospect of being alone with him. On a tropical island late at night, *both* of them legal, consenting adults.

Her imagination raced to places that made her blush.

It was definitely to her advantage that he believed she was cool enough to plot and plan and play a game. Now all she had to do was keep up the pretense.

It wouldn't be very hard to do, Shannen pep-talked herself, as she slowed her pace. She wasn't a giddy schoolgirl anymore, she was a mature woman known for her competence and self-control.

All she had to do was be herself—her *current* self. To tell Tynan Howe that this was the last time she would sneak around the island to meet him, and nothing he could say or do could change her mind.

That was all she had to do.

The moment Shannen spied Tynan Howe/Hale standing in the secluded grove of palm trees, the confidence-boosting tape she was playing in her head became a jumble of blather.

Fortunately, she had a moment or two to regain her composure before he sensed her presence. She knew he couldn't hear her approaching. The wind and the sounds of the nocturnal birds and animals provided ideal cover.

That secret moment or two also provided her with time to study him, and helplessly Shannen made a thorough mental inventory.

He was tall and tanned and muscular, and his *Victorious* crew T-shirt and loose khaki shorts emphasized his build to perfection. His face was all arresting masculine features: the coffee-colored brown eyes alert with intensity and intelligence, the strong jaw and sharp blade of a nose, the mouth well shaped and sensual.

His dark-brown hair was cut short, perhaps in concession to the island heat? She remembered he'd worn it longer nine years ago, when at twenty-five, he'd been a legal adult and she, only seventeen, was not.

Unbidden came a visceral pang of memory, that hungry yearning she'd felt back then every time she'd looked at him.

It was remarkably similar to what she was feeling right now.

Shannen was aghast. This was a mature woman known for her competence and self-control? She had to get out of here, and fast!

"Shannen," he called to her quietly.

Too late she realized she had accidentally moved into his line of vision. Okay, let's get this over with! She took a deep breath. "Hello, *Mr. Hale.*"

Her deep breathing had the unfortunate effect of making her sound throaty and breathless. That was certainly unintended. Shannen frowned.

"Do you disapprove of my alias?" Ty walked forward to meet her, his hands in his pockets, looking relaxed and cool and calm, everything she knew she was not.

She resented his composure mightily. "You can call yourself anything you want, it doesn't matter to me."

"I wonder who voted to oust Cortnee tonight?" Ty

stopped in front of her and attempted another conversational sally. "It seems obvious that Jed cast the vote against Konrad, but the vote against Cortnee came as a surprise."

Diverted, Shannen nodded her agreement. "I thought the five of us would unanimously vote against Jed, but there were only four votes against him. Enough to send him away, thank heavens. Maybe either Konrad or Rico decided they'd had enough of Cortnee?"

"Or you or your sister did," suggested Ty.

"We both voted against Jed. Bad enough he's an insufferable braggart, but hearing he's such a user totally clinched it."

"It's a secret ballot, so who knows? Unless you and Lauren discussed your votes?"

"We didn't have to. We can't stand Jed. And what a poor loser he was, throwing that big tantrum. It was pretty funny when Konrad couldn't stop laughing, though." Shannen smiled at the memory. "Konrad's been absolutely giddy today."

"The Internet discussion boards will be lit up over this," said Ty. "Jed does have a loyal following, who will be furious that he's out of the game. That vote against Cortnee will be dissected, too. She has her own fan base. And you and your sister have an even bigger one."

"We do?"

"Absolutely. Clark Garrett said you two are even being discussed on twins.com, which is normally used for parenting tips on multiple-born kids. He's elated with the scope of the show. Watch him try to find quadruplets for *Victorious II.*"

Shannen stared at him, completely nonplussed. "I haven't thought about public reaction to the show since the first few days after we arrived here. You're…keeping up with it?"

"You can't escape it in the crew's camp. Viewer response to *Victorious* is in the air we breathe there. Clark

Garrett is obsessed with the ratings, and he and Bobby monitor the show's Internet activity like overanxious mothers.''

She twisted her hands. ''It's strange how life in this game seems to be more real than real life back home right now.''

And it was downright unnerving how she had managed to fixate on him to the exclusion of real life back home! Shannen gulped.

''What is your real life like back at home, Shannen?'' He sounded genuinely interested.

She didn't want him to be. ''Haven't you read my *Victorious* bio? The basic facts are all there,'' she said glibly.

''The basic facts are pretty minimal. You and your sister graduated from West Falls University. You're a nutritionist at West Falls Hospital, and Lauren teaches home ec at West Falls High. You both were granted leaves of absence from your jobs to do this show—which you claim you tried out for as a lark. There isn't any real personal information.''

''Such as?''

''Mention of a boyfriend or fiancé.'' He cleared his throat. ''A child or ex-husband. That sort of thing.''

''Because there aren't any. Lauren and I are both happily single and free.''

Their eyes met. Ty was the first to look away. ''It's your turn to ask me,'' he said in a peculiar tone.

Shannen guessed he'd been trying to be wry but had ended up sounding sheepish instead. Best of all, he knew it. His discomfiture delighted her.

''I'm supposed to ask if you have a girlfriend or fiancée or wife and kids? No, I'll pass. I really don't care.''

''Don't you?''

He met her gaze again, and Shannen's pulses jumped. Sexual awareness crashed over her like a wave breaking on the shore. They were standing way too close, she realized with a start.

How had that happened? She had no recollection of either of them moving, yet they must have, because now they were in each other's personal space, within easy touching distance.

"I don't mind volunteering that I don't have a girlfriend, fiancée or wife and kids. No ex-wives, either," Ty said, breaking the brief charged silence.

"You Howes are so dedicated to honesty," she said sarcastically. "Such role models for morality! Oh wait, I forgot—you're a *Hale* now, you're keeping your true identity a secret. Which is just more Howe deception, if you ask me."

"You could look at it that way, I suppose. But my sister Jessie Lee and I see it from a different angle. She gladly and permanently dropped Howe for her married name. Jessie Lee says nobody in their right mind wants to carry the burden of the name Howe at this point in time. Well, I'm of sound mind, Shannen."

"Jessie Lee isn't the sister who embezzled the money from the flood relief fund, is she?"

"No, that would be Janice. Who is still serving time. She would disagree with Konrad about the tastiness of prison food, by the way."

"She had a trusted position with a respected charity organization, and she stole from the very victims she was supposed to be helping," Shannen said sternly. "She deserves to be in jail!"

"You won't get any argument about that from me." Tynan held up his hands in a gesture of truce. "My brother, Trent, took his rightful place there, too, after he almost singlehandedly brought down the biggest accounting firm in the country with his auditing schemes. Meanwhile, it's disturbing to consider what he might be cooking up in prison now, with all that time on his hands."

"There was a dreadful cousin, too," Shannen blurted out before she could stop herself. The Howe family's fall was not unlike a train wreck that you tried to avert your eyes from but couldn't help staring at anyway. "What finally happened to him?"

"Cousin Davis is locked up for a very long time. Between the postal service investigation and what they found on his computer, they nailed him cold, thank God." Ty sighed. "Being a Howe means serving as a target for numerous well-deserved potshots. Blame comes with the name, which is why I decided to use Hale."

"Because you're such a paragon of virtue?" she asked, baiting him.

"Because I didn't enjoy being a pariah by proxy. There are lots of people who believe that an uncorrupt Howe is an oxymoron, like a good terrorist."

"Are you going to be a Hale permanently?" Shannen was curious.

"I don't know. I do know that it's a great relief to be anonymous, something you've given up by being on this show. After the game is over and you're back home enduring the media attention, you'll—"

"Want to change my name to escape my notoriety? I seriously doubt it."

"Your name won't matter. Since you're visually known through TV exposure, you'll be identified on sight."

"Oh, well, how bad can that be?" Shannen gave a dismissive shrug. "As twins, Lauren and I have always been stared at. After this, a few more people will stare at us. Then we'll go back to work, interest in us will quickly fade and everything will return to normal."

"Maybe. Or maybe you'll win this game and be a millionaire, Shannen. That will surely change your life."

"Surely," she echoed mockingly. "Should I ask you in advance how to fend off fortune hunters? After all, you've been hounded by scheming gold diggers your entire privileged life, haven't you?"

He had the grace to look ashamed. "I knew it was too much to hope you'd forgotten...that."

"Being called a conniving gold digger and white-trash jailbait is rather memorable, Tynan."

He groaned. "Shannen, I never thought you were a—"

"Calculating fortune hunter? Of course you did. And to tell the truth, you were right about the appeal your money held for me. I liked the idea that you were very rich. I don't mind being called conniving, either. That's a compliment in some circles, and in this game it's crucial. But the jail-bait, white-trash part—ouch!"

She hoped she'd pulled off the breezy insouciance she was aiming for. She certainly wasn't feeling that way. His invective had seared her brain and remained engraved there ever since he'd hurled it at her the fateful night he'd broken her heart.

Shannen gave her head a quick shake. No, she wasn't going to stir up all those old feelings, not here, not now!

"I didn't mean it, Shannen." Ty's voice was low and urgent. "I was desperate that night, and I didn't trust myself around you. Remember, I'd just found out a few hours earlier that you were only seventeen years old."

He paused and shook his head ruefully. "From the first time I met you, your effect on me was nothing less than explosive and exciting, and the more we saw each other, the deeper my feelings grew. But then I saw you getting off that school bus. A school bus, Shannen! I couldn't believe it. I did some checking around and finally found out the truth. You were way too young for me. It was wrong for us to be together, and I knew I had to say something to make you... You were too young to understand what you..."

His voice trailed off.

Shannen found hers. "That's ancient history. I don't want to talk about it."

She was both fascinated and repelled by his unsteady pronouncement. Was it the truth, or was he indulging in some self-serving revisionist history?

Not that it mattered. Not that she cared at all.

He was a condescending, self-righteous jerk, she reminded herself, recalling how she'd hurled the epithet at him that same night. It was the most insulting thing her seventeen-year-old self could come up with while grappling with the pain of what he'd called her.

And it was lame compared to his pernicious insult. She had a far better verbal arsenal now.

"I suppose it would be boorish of me to point out that you were the one who brought it up in the first place with your fortune-hunter crack?" Ty's lips quirked.

"You were boorish to say it back then," she shot back. "But when faced with packs of fortune-hunting vixens, all's fair, I suppose. Still being relentlessly plagued by them?" she added caustically.

"Not anymore. Fortune-hunting vixens don't bother us fortuneless guys."

"Do you mean—did you— You lost all your money?" The notion was staggering.

Ty looked uncomfortable. "The family legal bills and penalty fines equaled the national budget of a small country. And let's not forget all those civil suits filed against us."

"But don't the rich have trust funds and all, that can't be touched?"

"When you have an enterprising auditing genius like Trent in the family, nothing is safe," Ty replied.

"Your brother stole from his own family, too? My brother has done the same thing." Shannen lowered her voice, as she always did when talking about her brother. As Gramma said, There were some things that didn't need to be shouted from the rooftops. Big brother, Evan, was one of them, even here, alone with Ty in the middle of the island.

"From the time Lauren and I first learned what money was, we learned that Evan would swipe it from us—pennies, nickels, dimes. He didn't care how small the amount—Evan would take it."

"Who would've expected we'd share a bonding moment over our thieving brothers?" Ty gave a hollow laugh before turning serious once again. "Shannen, there is no justifying what I said to you that night. At the time, I believed I was doing the right thing to keep you away from me, but since then—"

"Oh, spare me the tired old 'cruel to be kind' excuse." Shannen's temper flared. Their bonding moment, such as it was, was over. "It's phony and self-righteous and I don't buy it. Motives can be either cruel or kind but not both."

"Motives can definitely be mixed, Shannen."

Fast as a heartbeat, he backed her against the thick column of a palm tree. He slipped his arms around her, trapping her between himself and the tree.

"I'd like to know your motives in renewing our relationship." His voice was husky. "I'd be willing to bet my camera equipment that they're...mixed. Would I be right?"

With a soft gasp Shannen tilted her head back and looked up at him. The hot gleam in his dark eyes challenged her; his smoldering sexuality fueled hers. She felt her nipples tighten as sharp coils of desire spiraled deep inside her.

"I'm not trying to renew our relationship, because we don't have one," she said huskily. "We never did. I had a one-sided crush on you when you were a hotshot law student and I was a teenage idiot. End of story."

"It was more than that and you know it." Tynan nuzzled her neck, drawing her closer. "I was crazy about you, Shannen. When I found out you were just a kid, I felt like I'd been kicked in the gut."

Sensual hunger was swiftly infusing her body with hot, syrupy warmth. Shannen knew she should fight it, and she tried to bolster her resistance against it.

"I was still the same person you claimed to be so crazy about."

"Not even close, Shannen. I thought you were a twenty-two-year-old graduate student—because that's what you'd claimed to be. Quite a difference between that and a lying little teenager who was using me to rebel."

"I wasn't! Using you to rebel, that is," she specified, because she couldn't deny she had been a teenager or that she'd purposely lied about her age.

Right now she was feeling much the way she'd felt back then when he'd taken her in his arms. The same pounding excitement, the same fierce arousal.

Almost a decade later he still evoked a hormonal hurricane within her. It should have been a sobering realization, not a thrilling one.

But thrilling it was. She was aching to touch him, and finally, nervously she allowed herself to. Just a little, Shannen vowed, just this one last time before she returned to camp and never did this again.

She reached up to curve her hand around his jaw. He'd been clean shaven this morning—she had noticed, just as she did every day—but now a light stubble covered his jaw. It felt sensuous and scratchy and very erotic.

Her fingers slid to his mouth and traced his lips.

He caught her thumb with his teeth and gently pulled on it at the same time his big hand closed over her breast.

A moan escaped from her throat, and she felt herself slipping under his spell. *Again.* Ty was the first man ever to make her feel weak with wanting. Who would've guessed that in the nine years that followed their parting, he would remain the only man to elicit that response?

All those years her icy control had never wavered, and then along came Tynan, and once again she melted like a Popsicle in tropical sun. He held such power over her!

Sudden alarm bells began to sound in her head. With power went control, and all her adult life Shannen made sure that she was the one with both.

She hadn't been that way at seventeen, though. She'd

been all too willing to cede everything to Ty, "white-trash jailbait" that she'd been. Shannen winced.

He brushed his mouth over hers in a tempting, tentative caress. "We've been down this road before, Shannen."

Yes, they had. Shannen's alarm turned into panic. Was she nuts? Or maybe just "white-trash jailbait-all-grown-up," out for a midnight romp on the beach with the man who'd coldly dumped her when she was utterly vulnerable.

Ty lifted his head and gazed down at her. "But we never got far enough, did we, sweetheart? Tonight—"

"Nothing is going to happen tonight, either!"

He wasn't expecting it, so when she pushed at his chest with both hands, Shannen successfully shoved him away from her. He had to make momentary use of his arms to maintain his balance, and she took the opportunity to make her escape.

"I'm out of here. And don't try to...to contact me again," she ordered, gulping for breath. "I won't meet you again, no matter what."

Ty snaked out his arm in time to catch the tail of her cotton T-shirt. She kept walking, but he held firm. The shirt began to pull and stretch.

Shannen struggled and the material grew thinner. "Let me go!"

"No."

"You'll rip my shirt!" Her voice rose.

"Then you'd better stand still, hadn't you?"

The amusement in his voice struck an incendiary chord in her. "If you don't let go of my shirt right now, I'll sue you for...for sexual harassment. I'm not bluffing, Tynan *Howe!* Jed's threats to sue might have no basis, but mine will be—"

"Based on my name? Is that what your emphasis on Howe means, Shannen?" The coldness in his tone was reflected in his eyes. "'Your Honor, this man is a Howe, which makes him a sexual predator by blood.' Case closed.''

Ty let go of her shirt. Shannen meticulously smoothed out the material.

All she had to do was to agree with him, and he would leave her alone. It was easy enough, and she would get what she wanted, right?

She opened her mouth to speak, but no words came out.

Because she knew a thing or two about the pain and rage caused by an accusation that hit way too close to home. Like being called white trash when certain family members acted in a—well, what might be deemed a white-trashy way.

Shannen thought of her mother and brother and their never-ending bad behavior—the drinking and fighting at seedy bars, jumping from one rotten relationship to the next, bouncing checks while running up exorbitant credit-card debts. You could make a case that they were the low-rent version of the Howes, though Shannen wasn't interested in making it.

She and Lauren and their older sister, Jordan, had worked all their lives to be different from Mom and Evan, the Cullen reprobates.

Surprisingly, Ty's situation was much like her own, since he was a Howe by blood, though in behavior unlike them. He was certainly no sexual predator like his odious father and cousin. She couldn't accuse him of that.

And worse than any false accusation was her sinking realization that she wasn't sure she wanted him to leave her alone. She might not wish to have sex on the beach with him tonight, but that didn't mean she wanted to give up his attention.

It was enough to make anyone edgy!

Shannen crossed her arms in front of her chest and glowered. ''Playing the martyr doesn't suit you, Tynan.''

His lips curved into a slow smile. As if he knew why

she hadn't said what was guaranteed to send him on his way. "Is that what I was doing, Shannen?"

"Yes!"

"I guess it must've worked, though, because we're both still here."

"Only because—only until—" She spluttered, gave up and tried again. "Tynan, you can't demand that I meet you and expect me to—"

"It was a request," Tynan said, his voice deepening. "A polite one." They were close enough for him to rest both his hands on her shoulders. "And you came tonight because you wanted to, Shannen."

"No." She ducked out of his grasp. "I'm only here because—"

"You kissed me last night and you loved it?"

"*You* kissed *me!* And I...and you—" She broke off, her cheeks aflame. "Look, the only reason I'm here is to tell you to forget about last night. I admit I shouldn't have contacted you in the first place. That was a big mistake on my part. I...I wasn't thinking straight. We haven't been getting the proper nutrition here on this island, and it's affecting my brain."

"Nice try." Ty nodded his approval. "More original than the overused 'not guilty for reasons of insanity.' Not guilty for reasons of malnutrition, with you being a nutritionist, sounds downright credible. So, help me out, Shannen—what's *my* excuse for being here? I've been eating three square meals a day."

"Go ahead and brag about all the great food you get every day," she grumbled. "Describe every meal in detail. Torture me with tales of every bite."

"Now who's playing the martyr?" Ty grinned.

"Good night, Tynan. I'm going back to camp now. Hopefully, everybody is still sound asleep, or I'll have to pretend I've been, uh, using the facilities an awfully long time."

"Wait! Before you go." Ty caught her hand. "I brought you something." His thumb glided over her palm, then he lifted it and stared at the blisters. "From the rowing?" he asked, frowning with concern.

She nodded and disentangled her hand from his. "They hurt, and when the salt water touches them, I want to scream."

Ty examined her other hand. "I have some antibiotic salve I'll give you. It speeds up the healing and has a pain ingredient in it, too. Wait here and I'll go get it. I'll be back in less then ten minutes."

"But I can't—you can't—"

"While you're waiting, eat this." Ty handed her a plastic plate, removing the cover to reveal a sandwich made with thick Italian bread.

"It's turkey, cheese, lettuce and tomato," he said. "I brought you some cookies, too." He handed her a paper bag with two peanut butter cookies in it. "And a bottle of iced tea."

Shannen stared at the food—unexciting everyday items on the family dinner menu, but here, on the island, where acquiring food was part of the game, a priceless bounty.

And illicit.

"Isn't this cheating?" she whispered nervously, sitting down on the sand and eyeing the food with longing. Her stomach was growling noisily now.

"I'll get the ointment." Ty disappeared into the night, leaving Shannen alone with the meal.

Four

Shannen stared at the unexpected treasure he'd given her. She'd actually dreamed of food while on this island, and now here it was, literally, a dream come true.

She picked up the sandwich and sniffed it. Who would've thought that deli turkey, swiss cheese, tomato and lettuce could have such a heavenly aroma? And was that honey mustard spread on the bread? Oh, happy day!

Who would've believed that this sandwich could smell more wonderful than one of Gramma's freshly baked apple pies?

But it did—because it was here in her hand, and she could eat it right now if she wanted.

If she wanted? Oh, yes, she wanted to eat that sandwich! And the peanut butter cookies, too. Shannen put down the sandwich to sniff each cookie. She felt almost dizzy with pleasure, and she wasn't even a particular fan of peanut butter in any form.

There was the bottle of iced tea, too. Lemon-flavored,

and one of her favorite brands. She'd had nothing to drink on this island but the bottled water supplied by the crew for health reasons and some terrible coffee they'd won in a food contest early on. Jed had insisted on brewing it and had ruined it, much to the bitterness of the tribe.

That is, she and Cortnee, Rico and Konrad had been bitter and quite vocal about the ruined coffee. Lauren and the two earlier departees from the tribe, Lucy and Keri, had come to Jed's defense and all claimed the undrinkable swill was actually delicious.

"Are you Jed's groupies or something?" Rico had groused at the time, and Shannen, resenting the aspersion cast at Lauren, had glowered at Rico for the remainder of the day.

Now Shannen frowned again, thinking about that unexpected alliance. Lauren had claimed she'd sided with *them* to keep the numbers even, which meant keeping the peace. Shannen didn't understand Lauren's reasoning then, and she still didn't.

She gazed longingly at the food as she thought of her twin. She couldn't eat this food without sharing it with Lauren, she just couldn't. Her sister was just as hungry as she was.

She could take the food back and hide it near the spring, then wake up Lauren and share it with her. It was as if a little cartoon imp had perched on her shoulder, to whisper in her ear. There would be no cameras around to film them at this late hour. She and Lauren could enjoy their treat and no one would be the wiser.

But just as in a cartoon, another little voice—that of the angel who'd just arrived to perch on her other shoulder?— also had something to say. Something completely different from the devilish imp.

Eating this food would be cheating. Sharing it with Lauren would be dragging her sister into a conspiracy of dishonesty. And she would also have to add lying to Lauren to the list of her wrongdoings, because where could she say that this food had come from? A sandwich shop in the jungle?

If she were to truthfully tell Lauren that Ty had given it to her, Lauren would want to know why. Which would mean either confessing her past fling to her twin or making up some reason why chief cameraman Tynan Hale had decided to slip the Cullen sisters some food on the sly.

Shannen suddenly glanced around her, half expecting to see the cameras filming her. What if this was some sort of setup?

But she was all alone, and her stomach was churning in hungry anticipation.

To eat or not to eat. What a dilemma!

No, it wasn't a dilemma at all, lectured Shannen's invisible but vocal Little Angel. It was something far simpler—and way more dangerous.

This was temptation.

Shannen heaved a groan. Gramma had a lot to say about temptation down through the years and never hesitated to say it.

"If you keep off the ice, you won't slip through."

"You can't be caught in places you don't visit."

"If you don't touch the rope, you won't ring the bell."

Those three sprang instantly to mind; if she were to think another minute or two, she could come up with at least ten more in a similar vein.

And, of course, there was the unnerving one about giving the devil a ride. Shannen shuddered. Maybe it was because Mom and Evan had completely ignored Gramma's warnings and messed up their lives, that Shannen, Lauren and Jordan—sometimes called "the third twin" since she was only a year older—paid Gramma such careful heed.

Except for that brief, dizzying period in her life when Shannen had thrown out Gramma's wisdom and sneaked

around to meet Ty. No happy ending there. She hadn't
strayed from the straight and narrow since.

She wasn't about to do it now. Shannen stared out at the
dark ocean, leaving the food untouched. "If you don't take
a bite of the forbidden food, you won't be cheating."

She could pass down that one, her own personal version
of temptation shunned, to her own grandchildren...if she
ever had any.

Ty returned shortly afterward.

"Here's the ointment." Before she could say a word, he
knelt down beside her and smeared it on her right hand,
then her left.

The salve was thick and warm and soothed her blisters
on contact. Shannen immediately felt guilty.

"This isn't fair." She bit her lower lip. "The others—"

"I don't care about the others." Ty slipped his arm
around her shoulder. "Keep the ointment. Take it back to
the camp with you."

Shannen resisted laying her head against him. It would
be so easy to do that. Too easy. Instead, she shook off his
arm and struggled to her feet.

"You had that sandwich and cookies and tea with you
before I got here tonight. Is that why you told me to come
here, so you could give me food?" She was floored by the
sudden realization.

"And you thought I was just out for sex," Ty said wryly,
rising, too. "Of course, if you're willing, I'm—" He
paused, glancing at the uneaten food for the first time.

"You didn't eat it." He sounded disappointed.

"Gramma would say I'd be letting the devil in the cart
if I were to take one bite," mused Shannen.

"Relax. I promise you won't be held to the riding him
home part."

She resisted the urge to smile. "You heard me quoting
Gramma, hmm?"

"I filmed you quoting her, remember? I've heard a different version of the same theme—'Needs must when the devil drives.' I suppose that could be the Howe family credo, the true one. My mother should needlepoint it on one of those canvases she's forever working on. She's filled every room of the house with them made into pillows and pictures and foot stools and is still going strong.''

Shannen swallowed, unsure how to respond but feeling the need to say something. "I saw your mother on the news when your father resigned from Congress after the, uh, um, final incident. She looked incredibly calm. Maybe the needlepoint helps," she added quickly.

"No, it's the tranquilizers around the clock that keep her comfortably numb." Ty heaved a sigh. "Shannen, I'm not a devil and I don't want to lead you astray. It's just that I know you're hungry and I wanted you to have something to eat."

"Why?"

He turned his back to her to stare out at the sea. The white caps from the waves were the only breaks in the vast stretch of blackness. "Why wouldn't I?"

"No fair answering a question with a question. I'd like a straight answer. Why do you want to help me to cheat?"

"Not cheating, Shannen," he countered quickly. "It's more like—"

"Of course it's cheating, Ty. Don't go all Howe on me and get weaselly with words."

"Weaselly with words?" he repeated, as if unfamiliar with the concept.

"You know exactly what I mean, Ty. After all, your father's classic line, 'It depends on what is meant by a call girl ring,' is still quoted by politicians *and* comedians when—"

"Can we skip the quotes and the commentary, Shannen? If you don't want my help, just say so."

"I don't want your help, Tynan."

"Okay. I won't offer any more, then."

"And if you expect me to say 'thank you' for tonight, well, you can just—" She clenched her fists in frustration. "Would you kindly turn around when I'm speaking? I don't like addressing a person's back."

"I wasn't being intentionally rude, I was being… prudent." Ty slowly turned around. "But here we go again, anyway."

"What do you mean?"

"I mean we're doing it again. Picking an argument over nothing. Quarreling about anything. It's all an excuse to prolong our time together. And while fighting ought to keep us from touching each other, of course it won't. I predict we're moments away from another hot clinch."

"You are so far wrong, you're—" She had to catch her breath; his bluntness had physically winded her "—wrong!"

Very articulate, Shannen, she mocked herself. Why not call him a condescending, self-righteous jerk, too? Where are your allegedly superior verbal skills when you really need them?

"When you've filmed as many episodes of daytime television as I have, you know exactly what's going on here. Frustrated sexual tension. It's a staple on the soaps." He tilted her chin with his thumb and forefinger. "Unfortunately, we're caught in that same maddening trap."

Shannen gaped at him, uncertain what to address first. "You worked on a soap opera?"

"Three of them. It's where I got my start as a cameraman. I moved from daytime TV to primetime news magazines and the reality game shows. I've learned things on every job, and along with how to shoot close-ups of a person's best angle, I also picked up some true life lessons on the soaps."

"And you think we're like a soap opera couple?" Shannen laughed at that preposterous notion.

"Honey, we could *be* one. We even have the obligatory

conflict in our past.'' His fingers lazily stroked the slender column of her neck.

Shannen shivered, though it was pure heat streaking through her. She quickly stepped away from him, out of touching range.

''And don't you dare say I expect you to come after me and...and grab me. Because I don't!''

''So adamant.'' He laughed. ''I'm tempted to see what would happen if I did.''

''There's been enough temptation here tonight,'' scolded Shannen. ''And I'm ashamed of myself for even *considering* a bite of that food.''

She started walking back to the path. He followed her, placing his hand on the small of her back.

''It was extremely ethical of you not to eat that food, Shannen.'' His voice was thoughtful. ''I bet any of the others would've bolted it down without a single qualm.''

''Lauren wouldn't've touched it.'' Shannen stopped in her tracks so quickly he almost crashed into her. ''You'd better not go any farther. If someone sees you—''

''I'll turn around when we see the camp. And here, Shannen, don't forget this.'' He pressed the tube of ointment into her hand.

''This is cheating, too, Tynan.'' She dropped it, and it would've hit the sand if Ty, anticipating her reaction, hadn't caught it first.

''Share it with Lauren and Cortnee. I'm sure they have blisters,'' said Ty. ''Then you won't have any unfair advantage. Medicine falls into a different category than food. And I'm not using subterfuge—or weasely words.''

''They do have blisters, their hands are as bad as mine,'' Shannen admitted. ''I think Cortnee's are even worse.''

''Be sure that the three of you hold your hands up tomorrow so we can film them. We'll go in for some vivid close-ups.'' He smiled slightly. ''The viewing audience loves stuff like that, the ever-popular gross-out scenes.''

"Then they would've loved seeing Konrad barehandedly massacre that fish, but you didn't film it," she reminded him.

"True. I decided that Konrad and the murdered fish would be ideal for a show like *The World's Truly Disgusting Videos* but not for *Victorious.*"

"Clark Garrett would disagree. But I won't tell him about the fabulously nauseating footage he missed because you played censor."

"I felt I must. After all, we Howes are certainly the arbiters of good taste, among other things, are we not?" Ty was droll.

Or cynical. Or ashamed and quick to make a joke about his family's wretched reputation before anyone else did?

"Did you think I was going to toss off some Howe-related barb?" Shannen blurted her thought aloud.

She felt a pang of guilt. After all, she'd been quick to throw in the now-legendary statement made by his father when the news broke about the call girl ring being run out of Congressman Howe's office. As if that weren't scandalous enough, the congressman couldn't even plead ignorance to it all because he was getting a piece of the action himself, both financially and physically.

"I wouldn't blame you, I make them myself," Ty said laconically. "My family's antics were so outrageous, they turned themselves into cartoons who can only be comprehended by lampooning them. I wouldn't be surprised if the pope himself has told a Howe joke or two."

Shannen remembered how proudly Tynan had talked about his family nine years ago, before the Howes' infamous fall from grace. His father, the venerable congressman; his brother, the brilliant accounting executive who'd made his company stock a Wall Street darling. And the other Howes, seemingly equally gifted and talented, who'd turned out to be equally conniving and corrupt.

But back then the Howes had sounded like superbeings

to her, so very far removed from the Cullens, who eked out a livelihood from their West Falls diner. She had been so sure that Ty's true reason for breaking up with her had been based on class and status, not on her age. That it wasn't that she was too young for him, but not good enough for him, a wealthy, worthy Howe.

"It must've been—" she paused, searching for a tactful word but could do no better than "—strange for you, when everything…happened."

"It was strange when everything happened." He repeated her tortured attempt at diplomacy with a low rumble of laughter. "What's also strange is hearing you—Straight-Shooting Spitfire Shannen—suddenly go 'weaselly' with words."

He'd turned her own gibe back on her. He was deliberately provoking her. She should stalk off without a backward glance, after throwing the tube of ointment in his face.

But empathy for what had befallen him through no fault of his own kept her still. And standing there, she felt the heat emanating from his body, smelled his clean male scent.

She resisted a powerful urge to take the one step needed to close the small gap between them. To put her arms around him and lean against his solid warmth. To offer him comfort. And more…

She knew she couldn't, she shouldn't.

And she didn't. Frustration surged through her. She felt bone tired and suddenly hostile enough to start swearing.

Shannen looked down at the tube of ointment in her hand. "How am I supposed to explain where this came from? An all-night drugstore I found in the jungle?"

She heard the edge in her voice. That baiting, quarrelsome edge. As if she were trying to pick a fight with him.

To prolong their time together, to keep from touching him? Shannen jerked her head up and saw Ty watching her. The way he did when he was behind the camera. Always watching her.

He arched his brows.

She guessed what he was thinking. "We are *not* like a soap opera couple!" she snapped.

"If you say so." He gave her ponytail a quick tug. "Tell them you brought the ointment with you from home. Smuggled it in with your personal hygiene stuff."

"Lauren will know that I didn't."

"Say that you don't tell her everything. We both know that's the truth." He leaned down and lightly kissed her forehead. "Good night, Shannen. Sleep well."

"I will," she whispered after him.

"Lucky you. I know I won't."

"And remember, no more contact between us." Shannen's whisper, as adamant as it was soft, followed him as she walked away from him. "None at all. This is over, Tynan. You stay on your side of the camera and I'll stay on mine. Do you hear me? I mean it."

"I hear you, Shannen." His soft laughter echoed in the tropical night.

His laughter was long gone by the time he reached his tent. Ty clutched the rejected bottle of iced tea in his hand; he'd left behind the sandwich and cookies for whatever jungle scavenger should happen to find them. Unlike Shannen, the gulls or animals wouldn't turn down free food.

He'd begun to ruminate over her refusal to accept the meal during his late-night walk across the island. How she had resisted the temptation to eat, though he knew how hungry she was.

Why do you want to help me to cheat? Her words kept replaying in his head like the maddening hook of an advertising jingle.

Worse, he faced the fact that until she'd refused the food and made her pointed reproach, he hadn't considered what he'd done to be cheating at all. What he'd wanted to do was to help her. Period.

She was hungry and he wanted to feed her was the way he'd seen it from the moment he issued his decree for her to meet him tonight. If she should end up in his arms, so much the better, but his primary motive had been to give her food and drink.

To help her cheat.

Ty grimaced. Was this how it started for the others in his family? Doing something that seemed perfectly reasonable—even good!—when it was obvious to others from the start that it wasn't?

Did the Howes possess a defect in the ethics gene? Or was it an insidious element absorbed from growing up a Howe. His honesty gene could be afflicted, too.

Maybe that would explain why he had lied to Shannen about losing all his money. He and his mother and sister Jessie Lee all remained independently wealthy despite the rest of the family's travails, thanks to their own irrevocable trust funds.

Or had his reply been a self-protective response after hearing Shannen admit she'd liked the idea that he was very rich? Her words resounded in his head and he still wasn't sure if she'd been serious or sardonic when she uttered them.

From the time he had first learned that some people were nice to you only because they wanted what your money could buy—be it candy or baseball cards or jewelry or a luxurious life as a pampered wife—Ty had been on the alert.

Who knew if he'd been dishonest or cautious when he told Shannen that whopper tonight? Certainly he didn't.

Nature versus nurture. Had that conundrum ever been solved? He should offer himself up to be studied, Ty thought grimly. For the past seven years—since the first family scandal broke, bringing down the others in turn like a crashing line of dominoes—he had seen himself as a good Howe. The one too good to be saddled with the perfidious

Howe name, so he'd become a Hale, determined to make it a name to be proud of.

He wasn't feeling proud of himself now. Shannen wanted to win *Victorious* fairly, and though it had been unintentional, he'd tried to sabotage her.

But had it been unintentional? The question rocked him. Had he deliberately tempted her because he didn't want her to win? And was he also testing her by pretending he'd lost his portion of the Howe fortune? After all, she was in this game to win a million dollars. He'd been filming what she was willing to go through to get it.

He did want Shannen to win, Ty insisted to himself. Or more precisely, he didn't want to see her hurt, and it surely would be hurtful for her to be voted out of the game.

But if she were to win…

He could envision the aftermath of a win easily, simply by recalling past winners in the early popularity days of the reality game shows. The winner would be whisked between New York and Los Angeles for appearances on TV talk and radio shows. There might be offers from companies to star in commercials. If the winner was a girl, a plethora of men's magazines would dangle plenty of cash as an incentive to pose nude.

Ty's blood chilled at that thought. Cortnee could accept a nude centerfold offer and he wouldn't blink an eye; he wouldn't even buy the issue. But if Shannen were to pose nude…

He pulled off his clothes and threw them on the ground, cursing as he swung himself down on his hammock to lie inside his sleeping bag.

For the past nine years Shannen had been lost to him, and now that he'd found her again, now that he knew she felt something for him—and her responses to him definitely told him that—he was not going to share her with zillions of slavering males who pinned a nude layout of her on their walls.

He closed his eyes, picturing her naked. A sweet torture that guaranteed he wouldn't be falling asleep anytime soon.

As he lay there, common sense eventually reasserted itself. Shannen wouldn't pose nude for any magazine. She wouldn't take a nibble of a sandwich when she was hungry and she wouldn't strip naked for a centerfold layout.

But if she won the game, her life would definitely change from her current one as a hospital nutritionist in the small town of West Falls. She claimed it wouldn't, but he knew otherwise.

Money changed everything. And why would a beautiful young woman, enjoying a taste of fun-filled celebrity, want to make room in her life for *him?*

He might use the name Hale, but Shannen knew the disreputable truth about his family. Jessie Lee had been right on target when she'd said that nobody in their right mind would want to carry the burden inflicted by the scandal-ridden, joke-provoking name Howe.

Not only was Shannen in her right mind, she had done quite well without him since they'd parted.

And now, just as their relationship was heating up, the game was ending. Their time together on the island was drawing to a close.

Would she agree to even see him, when the game was over?

Possibly…if she lost. Fame was fleeting and fickle when it came to winners and losers. If she were merely one of the losers, instead of The Winner, he would at least have an opportunity to convince her that she wanted him—Tynan *Hale*—in her life.

If she won…

Ty thought of all the new people she would meet, the new *men* she would meet. Men who hadn't called her ''white-trash jailbait''—a slur she clearly couldn't forget; men who didn't come saddled with a name and family eponymous with corruption and public disgust.

If Shannen won *Victorious,* she would be lost to him again, this time forever. The more he considered it, the more Ty was convinced that was true.

No more contact between us. This is over. I mean it, she'd said tonight, and though he'd glibly replied that he heard her, Ty knew he hadn't, not really, not until right now.

Now the impact of her words reverberated within him. She was ending their relationship before it had a chance to evolve into intimacy, exactly what he had done nine years ago. He hadn't relented then; he couldn't have. Didn't she understand that?

He mentally argued his case against making love to a seventeen-year-old girl. Maybe if he'd been a seventeen-year-old boy, the playing field would've been even, but he had been a responsible adult....

So he'd stuck to his decision back then.

Suppose that Shannen stuck to hers, whether winning or losing this game. And just in case that wasn't torment enough, he could also ponder the timing of her "no more contact" edict.

She had issued her decree after he'd informed her that he was no longer rich. Suppose he had said yes, his inheritance remained intact, and that due to savvy investing, he was even richer today than he had been nine years ago? That he worked as a cameraman because it was interesting and challenging, not because he needed the job to pay his bills?

Would she have been open to "more contact" if she'd known that?

Five

"Ty, what'd you think about that shocker revelation last night? You know, that Jed secretly slept with both Keri and Lucy and then voted against them, like it meant nothing to him? Which it probably didn't, the rat!" By the sound of her voice, production assistant Heidi was highly indignant.

Ty was testing camera angles, adjusting light filters while waiting for the twins to emerge from their tent. Heidi flitted around him like a manic mosquito, talking nonstop, holding his coffee for him.

He said nothing, hoping she would take the hint and keep quiet. It was barely dawn—he'd slept about a total of an hour last night, and he hadn't given a single thought to the "shocker revelation" about Jed, Keri and Lucy.

With a long-suffering sigh, he reached for his coffee. Heidi handed it to him, chatting all the while. He'd obviously been too subtle with his hint; she hadn't picked it up.

"The other PAs, Kevin, Adam and Debbie—think it's possible that Cortnee made it all up, to turn the others against Jed," continued Heidi. "I mean, the fact she's still in the game when she's never been able to do anything to help win a single contest, and that she seemed like such an airhead at the beginning—well, I guess this proves that she's not, doesn't it?"

Heidi waited expectantly for Ty to answer. Since he hadn't been paying attention to a thing she'd said, all he could offer was, "Huh?"

"Cortnee turned out to be shrewd," explained Heidi. "She figured that Jed would talk the others into voting her out, so she had to strike first. Saying Jed had sex with Keri and Lucy guaranteed that the twins would turn on him. Did you see the looks on their faces when Cortnee dropped her bombshell? Shannen looked ready to puke in disgust, and Lauren—well, she was devastated, poor thing."

The mention of the twins immediately caught Ty's attention. He well knew Shannen's "ready-to-puke-in-disgust" look but, "Lauren was devastated?" he echoed. He'd definitely missed that.

"Well, yeah. It's obvious Lauren has this big crush on Jed, and to hear that he—"

"You're sure it's not Shannen with the crush?" Ty cut in, feeling his face flame with horror. He sounded like an insecure eighth-grader!

He was truly drowning in the rocky seas of lovesickness with that inane question. He knew Shannen didn't have a crush on Jed, yet he couldn't stop himself from seeking reassurance that she didn't. Oh, he was a lovesick fool, all right!

But Heidi thought he was making a joke, and she laughed obligingly. "Some crush that would be! Shannen usually looked at Jed like she wished she could dismember him."

"She looks at a lot of people that way," murmured Ty. Himself included, at times.

"Yeah, she does. But Lauren's so sweet, and remember

how she'd just gaze at Jed and praise him and stand up for him when the others dumped on him? There was no mistaking which twin was which when it came to Jed.''

"Do you think Shannen knows her sister has this crush on Jed?" asked Ty, his interest so piqued that he didn't bother to ponder what would've previously been unfathomable to him—that he would ever stand around eagerly gossiping with a production assistant.

"That's what we'd all like to know!" cried Heidi. "If you stop and think about it, we've never heard a personal conversation between the twins in the whole time we've been filming. We know all kinds of things about the others because they talk about themselves all the time. But the twins—zip, nada, nothing."

"Aside from mentioning the diner their family owns and occasionally quoting their grandmother, neither one has revealed anything about herself or her sister," Ty agreed.

Though he was glad Shannen didn't feel the need to bare her soul in front of the cameras, it was driving him crazy that she didn't feel the need to bare her soul to him away from the cameras, either. She remained a closed book, one he wanted to open.

"The twins just stick to making comments on what's happening on the island," said Heidi. "Do you think they're hiding something?"

"Um, hard to say," he mumbled. Shannen was already keeping a lot of secrets—their past relationship, his true identity, their clandestine meetings in the island grove. But was she hiding something *else?*

"Kevin says the twins are masters of deception," Heidi reported.

"Maybe not deception." Ty's tone was thoughtful. "But certainly discreet. Their personal conversations obviously take place when the cameras aren't around."

"Wouldn't it be cool to shoot a scene of Shannen asking Lauren about Jed?" enthused Heidi. "I wish there was a way for us to interact with them and suggest it, but then we'd be accused of interference and get fired. Oh, look, here comes—'' A twin emerged from the tent. ''—one of them, although I can't guess which.''

Ty knew exactly who it was. Lauren. He filmed her going to the spring for her morning ablutions, all the while anticipating the pleasure and pain of seeing Shannen again. The two feelings had become so intertwined, he could hardly separate them.

But as an endlessly long hour passed, his anticipation was supplanted by mind-numbing boredom.

The contestants noticed Shannen's absence, too.

''I can't believe your sister is still sleeping,'' said Konrad.

He, Rico and Cortnee sat around the fire with Lauren, their cups filled with the morning brew of boiled water flavored with two used tea bags shared among them. Breakfast was always the leanest meal of the day.

''You don't think she's, like, dead, do you?'' Rico sounded only half-jesting. ''Maybe someone ought to check on her.''

''She's sick,'' declared Cortnee. ''She was gone a really, really, really long time last night. When she came back, she sounded like she was gagging or sobbing or something. I asked her if she was okay and she said yes, but I didn't believe her.''

Ty almost dropped his camera. Shannen had been sobbing—as in crying? He watched the entire production crew come alive with curiosity and felt the protective urge to drive them away. So he could go to Shannen inside that pitiful tent and...

Shannen crawled out of the tent at that moment.

''Shannen!'' Lauren jumped to her feet and rushed over to her twin. ''Cortnee said you were sick last night. Why didn't you wake me up?''

Quick as lightning, Reggie Ellis moved in with his camera for a super close-up.

Shannen's actions were just as swift and instinctive. She put her hand over the camera lens. "Get that thing away from me," she ordered, "and don't ever shove it in my face again."

A stunned Reggie stopped filming and stared mutely at the equally amazed contestants and crew.

"Cut!" ordered Ty, who was the senior crew member at the camp at this early hour. It was an unnecessary command, since both Reggie and Paul, the only two with cameras besides himself, weren't shooting anyway.

Ty walked over to Shannen. "Are you all right?" he asked quietly, restraining the urge to touch her arm, her face, her hair, just to have some physical contact with her, however slight.

But he knew how much she wouldn't welcome that, not with all the onlookers.

"I'm fine, thank you for asking." Purposefully she stepped away from him and turned to Reggie. "I'm sorry. I, um, I guess I lost it for a minute there. You can start the cameras rolling again."

Reggie and Paul looked uncertainly at Ty.

"You better do what she says," Konrad interjected, a trifle gleefully. "It's cool the way she bosses you camera guys around like she's Clark Garrett herself."

For the first time Ty considered the implications of Konrad being part of their unfilmed interaction in the ocean the other day. Would Konrad use it to somehow discredit Shannen? And if so, would Shannen blame Ty for it all? He frowned.

"What do you think, Ty?" asked Reggie, rousing him from his troubling reverie.

"Go ahead." Ty nodded to the two other cameramen, and they all resumed shooting.

There was an awkward silence before Rico's acting experience came to the fore, picking up the scene where they'd left off.

"So, you were sick last night, but you didn't wake up your sister for help?" Rico cued Shannen. Her outburst could be seamlessly edited out if The Powers That Be so decided.

"I was accosted by a germ last night." Shannen spit out the words as if she had contempt for them, glaring directly at Ty, whose camera, of course, was on her. "But that's over with—I got it all out of my system. No need to drag anybody else into it."

Shannen met his eyes, sending him a not-so-subtle message. That he was the "germ" she'd gotten out of her system. She looked, she sounded, like she meant every word.

But Cortnee had said she'd heard Shannen crying last night. And by the looks of her this morning, by her uncharacteristically late awakening, Ty guessed that Shannen had spent a hellish, sleepless night, similar to his own. The notion pleased him. He was still very much in her system.

He smiled at her.

She stiffened. "I found this." She tossed the tube of antibiotic ointment to Cortnee. "You and Lauren should put it on your blisters."

"Can I use it?" Rico piped up. "I have blisters, too."

Blister-free Konrad cast him a scornful glance, then turned to Shannen. "Where did you find it?" he asked suspiciously.

"At the spring. Somebody must've dropped it. My guess is a member of the crew." Shannen's tone was challenging, as if daring someone to come up with another explanation. "I used it last night and it did help." She held up her hands to Ty's camera to show the partially healed blisters. "See?"

Did anybody detect the taunting note in her voice? Ty wondered. On the other hand, how could anyone miss it?

He saw the production assistants exchange inquiring glances.

Reggie and Paul dutifully shot the others rubbing the ointment on their painfully blistered hands. Shannen went to the spring to wash up, followed by Ty and his camera.

And Heidi. Her presence prevented any private conversation between Ty and Shannen.

It was frustrating, it was maddening. Shannen followed the rules of the game, ignoring the crew as if they were invisible. As if they weren't human beings. She washed her face and brushed her teeth and braided her hair into one thick plait, all at an interminably slow pace.

Ty felt Heidi shifting restlessly beside him and knew she was bursting to ask Shannen something about Lauren's crush on Jed. He shook his head forbiddingly at her.

Shannen intercepted the look.

"It looks like he's trying to incinerate you with that glare of his. What did you do to make him mad?" Shannen asked Heidi. "Or is he one of those bad-tempered bosses who gets ticked off for no reason at all?"

Ty noted that her friendly tone was at odds with the demonic glint in her eyes.

Heidi was dumbstruck at being addressed by a contestant. "I...I can't talk to you!" she gasped. "I could lose my job."

"You'd fire her?" Shannen addressed Ty this time. "Or rat her out to somebody else who would?"

"Don't worry, Heidi, I've turned off my camera," said Ty, but his eyes were holding Shannen's. "You aren't going to be fired."

"Thanks, Ty." Heidi gulped.

"You're a real prince, *Ty*," said Shannen. "So thoughtful, so concerned."

"I think I'd better go back to the camp and see if anybody needs me," Heidi said nervously. "Bobby should be arriving at any time now, and if it's okay with you, Ty, I'll just—''

"Sure. Go on back, Heidi." Ty was magnanimous. "I'll hold down the fort here."

Heidi left, giving him a look of gratitude mixed with sympathy, presumably for having to stay behind.

Shannen noticed. "Seems like your lackey feels sorry for you being stuck here with the Wicked Witch of the Island."

"You've terrified the poor girl," Ty said dryly. He set his camera down on the flat rock, giving up even the pretense of filming. "No fair dragging innocent bystanders into our own private war, Shannen."

"We're not at war," she snapped. "We're not anything."

"I'm merely the 'germ' you've gotten out of your system?" Ty laughed softly. "Liar."

Shannen clenched her fists at her sides. "You'd better pick up that camera and turn it on, or I'll get you fired."

"A smooth liar, too. Look how you handled the questions about the tube of ointment. You were so believable that the PAs will be in a frenzy wondering which one of them dropped it and if they'll be in trouble for it."

"I'm not a liar. Lying doesn't come naturally to me," she retorted.

"I see. Unlike the Howes, who have an inborn talent for lying, you've had to work to acquire the skill. But from your flawless impersonation of an over-twenty-one grad student to your ointment tale nine years later, it's obvious that you've mastered the art."

Shannen stalked off, only to return as if she were attached to some invisible string that Ty could pull as he pleased. It was almost too true; she'd wanted to get away from him, yet here she was, right back at his side. Making excuses as to why.

"After I deliberately didn't say anything about the Howes and their multitude of lies, you—"

"I understand. Howes and lying...too easy a target. Why bother?"

In spite of herself, she laughed. And quickly caught herself. "It's not funny, Ty. You don't always have to make the first joke about your family to fend off—"

"—the inevitable joke to be made by someone else? It's become a defensive habit, I guess."

"And it's not fair to keep referring to...what I did nine years ago. I was young and immature back then. I shouldn't have lied about my age and all, I know that."

"Then do you forgive me for doing the only thing I could back then, given those circumstances, Shannen?" he pressed, his dark gaze intense.

She averted her eyes. "Yes, but it doesn't matter anymore. We can't go back to the past. It's been too long, and we're different people now. I meant what I said last night, Tynan. We can't—"

"Cortnee said she heard you crying last night," Ty interrupted her again. "Were you?"

"No! And even if I was crying, it doesn't mean that it would have anything to do with you!" Shannen countered crossly. "Don't flatter yourself into thinking otherwise."

Ty stared at her. "I just had a thought."

She opened her mouth to speak, then shook her head. "Too easy a target. Why bother?"

They both grinned spontaneously.

Then Ty became intent. "Shannen, was it you Cortnee heard crying last night? She never mentioned you by name, and she can't tell you and Lauren apart. Did she actually hear Lauren crying? Is that why you're so upset this morning, Shannen?"

His face softened, and this time he gave in to the need to touch her. He laid his hand on her forearm, his fingers stroking lightly.

"Did you get back to camp last night, still hungry after staving off temptation, only to find Lauren crying her eyes out over Jed? That's more than enough to cause a sleepless night and to make you wake up in a ferocious mood."

"What?" Shannen's voice rose to a squeak. "What are you talking about? Why would Lauren cry over *Jed?* That jerk? *Please!*"

"Oh."

It occurred to Shannen that he was still stroking her arm. And that she was enjoying it way too much. She swatted his hand away. "What do you mean 'Oh'?" she demanded.

"Nothing." He shrugged. "Just 'Oh.'"

"You stand there looking totally clueless after making accusations about my sister and that narcissistic creep Jed but you—"

"I wasn't making an accusation. The production assistants all claim Lauren has a crush on Jed and that she looked devastated when Cortnee said he'd slept with those two other girls. I didn't see any devastation, so I thought I'd missed the crush, as well." His eyes narrowed perceptively. "Did you miss it all, too, Shannen?"

"Lauren wouldn't like a preening, self-absorbed twit like Jed," she insisted.

But a note of doubt had crept into her voice.

"Lauren could've been the one to cast the vote against Cortnee," said Ty. "In fact, she *must* have been the one. There was no reason for Rico or Konrad to vote against her, and you said that you didn't."

"Maybe Jed voted against Cortnee. She's been really bitchy toward him lately."

"But then who voted against Konrad?" countered Ty. "It had to be Jed. He was convinced Konrad did something to make the boat sink. I agree, but there's no proof—"

"It's irrelevant who voted against Cortnee, Ty." It was Shannen's turn to interrupt. "All that matters is that Jed was voted off. But I'll prove you're wrong about Lauren's supposed crush. I'll ask her about it. When we're alone and the cameras aren't around," she added pointedly.

"I wouldn't expect it to be any other way, especially given your penchant for secrecy—I mean, privacy."

"By the snarky way you said 'privacy,' I know you really did mean secrecy. In a negative way," she added tersely.

"Not negative. Curious. You and Lauren never share any personal information about yourselves. We can recite Cortnee's musical triumphs from grade school on, we've heard all about Konrad's prison adventures and Jed's wilderness adventures and Rico's—"

"Is that how the crew spends their off time?" Shannen interrupted. "Gossiping about the contestants?"

"Pretty much," he admitted. "But I didn't listen until they mentioned you and your sister. You're the only one on this island I'm interested in, Shannen. Now go ahead and throw it back in my face." Ty laughed ruefully. "I've set it up for you."

"When you put it that way, any retaliatory zinger I might make loses its—" Shannen paused, grimacing "—zing."

"With that kind of encouragement, I may as well bare my soul," Ty said wryly. "Well, why not? At this point I have nothing to lose."

Shannen felt her stomach do a Flying Wallenda-type somersault. And then Ty reached for her hand and gently tugged her toward him. She went, unresisting, squinting against the sun. Trying to stay immune to the urgency, the desire in his eyes.

"I know we can't go back to the past and that we're different people now, but that's a good thing, Shannen. I want to move ahead, not backward." Ty's voice was deep and low.

"I was actually glad to hear Cortnee say you were crying last night, because maybe it meant that you didn't really mean what you said when you left me. That you didn't want it to be over between us—to be over before anything had really begun,'' he added, as if expecting her to jump in to correct him.

He slipped behind her, brushing her body with his, in slow, sensual motion.

Shannen knew she was incapable of any kind of verbal gymnastics at this point. He was hypnotizing her with his tone, with his big hand that had begun to caress the bare skin of her back, between the end of her halter and the low waistband of her shorts.

''I hoped that what you really meant was that we should call some kind of moratorium until the game is over.'' The heels of his palms massaged her shoulder blades, and she tried to stifle a small moan of sheer pleasure.

Tried and failed. Her eyelids fluttered shut.

''We'll make plans to see each other after the game, to continue what we've begun. To be together.'' He lowered his mouth to her neck, flicked his tongue against her skin. ''I want us to be together, Shannen. I want you to want that, too.''

She didn't reply. Talking required too much thought, too much effort, and she didn't want to break the spell. Instead she inclined her neck to give him better access, shivering in pleasure at the feel of his lips, his breath against her hair. Didn't actions speak louder than words, anyway?

He whispered her name again and glided his hands around to the front of her, cupping her breasts with sensual care. He teased her nipples through the cotton of her halter, and she felt them tighten almost immediately. She pressed against his palms, encouraging, demanding.

This was what she wanted, what she needed. Ty, his touch, his voice murmuring what he wanted to do, what they would do together. Her defenses, already weak against him, crumbled. And she didn't care.

Suddenly, being caressed wasn't enough—she had to touch him, too. To kiss him the way she'd been dying to.

Shannen turned quickly and grasped his shirt, pulling him even closer, lifting her head as he lowered his to hers.

Their kiss was explosive, devouring. He held her head, burying his fingers in her hair as she clutched him, their tongues caressing, mating in erotic simulation.

They kissed long and hard, their bodies locked together, passion running hot and unrestrained. Shannen felt her knees buckle and she let Ty fully support her, knowing if he were to let her go, she'd fall. She was heady with sensual weakness and gave in to it, savoring it.

When Ty began to slowly, carefully lower them both to the ground, she clung to him, trembling with anticipation.

"Is there a hidden camera filming all this?" The voice, sounding exactly like Shannen's, filled the air. "Because the only camera I see is on a rock, and it's definitely not being used."

The sweet illusion of intimacy surrounding the lovers abruptly shattered.

Shannen pulled away first, and for a moment Ty stood there befuddled. He swore he'd heard Shannen's voice, but that couldn't be. His lips had been covering hers, his tongue deep in her mouth.

"Lauren." Shannen inhaled a breathless gulp of air.

Ty's head cleared and he opened his eyes. "Busted," he muttered.

"And then some," agreed Lauren. Ty blinked. She didn't sound as sweet as she usually did; her tone had an edge that was definitely Shannen-esque.

"What the hell is going on here, Shannen?" Lauren demanded, an auditory dead ringer for Shannen, as well as a visual one.

Shannen cast a covert glance at Ty. He nodded his head, giving her the go-ahead to tell all. In fact, he wanted Shannen's twin sister, the person closest to her, to know the whole truth about their relationship. Past, present and future.

Shannen bit her lip and looked down at the sand, seemingly disinclined to say anything. She needed time to regain her composure, Ty thought tenderly. Well, she could count on him to step in and explain everything.

"Shannen and I know each other," he began, giving Lauren his warmest we're-going-to-be-friends smile.

"Duh!" Lauren snapped. "I figured that out in the ocean yesterday, but I didn't know just how well you two 'know each other.'" She turned to her twin. "He gave you that ointment, didn't he, Shannen?"

Shannen nodded. "It's not truly cheating, I shared it with everybody," she said in a plaintive tone Ty had never before heard her use. "And he hasn't given me anything else, honest!"

"Not for lack of trying, obviously." Lauren was sarcastic.

"Look, let me—" Ty interjected, but both sisters ignored him.

"Shannen, we've come this far, we're almost down to the Final Four. One of us could actually win the whole game," cried Lauren. "We could win the million dollars! Why would you risk screwing things up like this?"

Shannen heaved a sigh. "I wasn't thinking, Lauren."

"Tell me something I don't know, Shannen," Lauren retorted acidly.

"You could plead not guilty by reason of malnutrition, Shannen," suggested Ty in an attempt to lighten the tension.

A mistake, he realized as the twins both glowered at him.

"Stay out of this, Tynan." Shannen's tone was sharp, dismissive.

"Sweetie, I'm in as deep as you are." He meant to sound cajoling and was surprised to hear the mockery in his tone.

Well, not too surprised. He was getting impatient, not to mention all that raging sexual frustration surging through him. Why wouldn't Shannen simply tell her sister the truth?

They hadn't committed a crime; they were two people in love.…

That rogue flash of insight struck him with the precision of a stun gun. He knew he wanted Shannen, that she intrigued and attracted him as much as she had nine years ago. More. But he hadn't thought of himself as in love with her. When was the last time he'd been in love?

For that matter, when was the *first* time?

Howes didn't fall in love; they had relationships that invariably soured, whether those involved were married or not.

This time Ty felt as if he'd been hit over the head with a shovel. He'd followed the standard Howe emotional blueprint by lying to Shannen about his financial status because he didn't fully trust her not to want him for his money.

And yet he thought he was in love?

Ty remembered that long-ago "coming of age" talk his father had given him and Trent.

"You'll be hearing all sorts of nonsense about love from girls." Dear old Dad had snickered, not bothering even to try to keep a straight face. "Don't be chumps and fall for it. The only kind of genuine love that can exist between opposite sexes is the mother and son and father and daughter kind. Possibly sister and brother. But so-called romantic love is pure fiction and don't forget it. Men and women get together for either sex or convenience, and don't be duped into thinking otherwise."

Ty winced at the memory. Well, when it came to his feelings for Shannen, he could safely rule out convenience. But sex was an integral part of their relationship. Was that all it was between them? A hot sexual infatuation fueled by the lush tropical setting, plus the enticing element of the forbidden?

Shannen must think so; she certainly wasn't pouring out her abiding love for him to her sister.

"Pick up that camera and start filming us," one of the twins said.

Ty blinked. Which one had spoken, Shannen or Lauren? For the first time he was unsure.

"I'll start talking about how hungry I am for the fabulous silver dollar pancakes at the diner," said Shannen. "We might as well get in a little free advertising for Gramma."

One telltale sign clued Ty that it was Shannen who was speaking; her lips were still moist and swollen from their kisses. But that startling moment when he couldn't tell one sister from the other jarred him. It seemed symbolic. Of exactly what, he wasn't sure. Right now he was sure of nothing at all.

"Okay," agreed Lauren. She picked up the camera and handed it to Ty.

He didn't turn it on. "You're one superb actress, Lauren," he said lightly. "After all those hours of filming, this is the first and only time I've ever seen you lose your temper or even display a hint of aggravation. Who knew that beneath that sweet serene exterior is—"

"Lauren *is* sweet and serene," Shannen jumped to her twin's defense. "She only gets upset when she's with me."

"You mean she'll only allow you to see how she *really* feels," corrected Ty. "Everybody else gets the Lady Lauren facade. As a control freak, your sister beats you hands down, Shannen." He laughed. "I feel privileged to see the true inner Lauren. Makes me feel like family."

Lauren look at him, aghast. "Shannen, what have you done?" she wailed. "I can tell that we can't trust this guy. He could make us lose the game. And we're so close, I can almost feel that money!"

"Ah, the sweet feel of cold hard cash." Ty's dark eyes glittered. "I can relate. You, too, hmm, Shannen?"

Shannen shot him a glare and caught Lauren's hand, dragging her away to join the others back at camp. Ty followed them, his camera rolling.

Six

Bobby Dixon showed up later in the day with food, money and another contest.

"Today we're going to have an auction. I'm going to give each of you five one-hundred-dollar bills. You can bid on all of these savory delights and spend as much as you want on anything you want—until your money runs out."

With a flourish, he unveiled an array of food: a cheeseburger with choice of condiments, a piece of chocolate cake topped with whipped cream and hot fudge, an enormous fresh fruit salad and a turkey sandwich on thick fresh bread.

Shannen's eyes connected with Ty's over that one. She felt her stomach rumble because she knew exactly how that sandwich smelled and could imagine how it tasted. Ty merely smiled, and she looked away, scowling.

Bobby was offering more food to be auctioned. A large bag of potato chips and a cold beer, a liter bottle of cola, a plate of nachos, a barbecued chicken, a tub of potato salad. A movie theater counter's assortment of candy. A container of fruit-flavored yogurt, a container of frozen yogurt. A quart of designer ice cream packed on dry ice so it wouldn't melt before the bidding concluded.

"If we have any cash left over after bidding, can we keep it?" asked Konrad, fondling the stiff new hundred-dollar bills.

"Sure," Bobby assured him smoothly. "But I sincerely doubt anybody will have any money left. Did I tell you I also have a steak dinner, complete with baked potato and salad with the dressing of your choice? And I'll throw in whatever you want as a beverage to go with it."

Rico gasped. "I bid three hundred dollars on the steak dinner."

"I bid three-hundred-fifty," said Konrad.

The twins exchanged glances.

"Red meat, ick!' exclaimed Cortnee. "I'll bid one hundred for the fruit salad. And fifty for the frozen yogurt."

The auction unfolded at a lively pace, with the cameras filming each contestant avidly devouring what they'd won.

Except for the Cullen twins. Neither bid on anything. Both stared resolutely at the five one-hundred dollar bills they held in their hands.

Ty noticed right away, of course. Amid the auction hoopla, it took the others a while longer.

"Shannen, Lauren, you haven't bid on anything yet," Bobby Dixon exclaimed at last, his dimples deeper than ever. "Let me tempt you with this—a monster BLT, with a pile of crisp bacon, fresh lettuce and tomato on the bread of your choice."

"No, thanks. Gramma makes the world's ultimate BLT at the diner," Shannen said blithely. "I wouldn't want to settle for anything less."

"N-not even here, when you're starving on an island?" Bobby's dazzling smile faltered a bit, but he quickly recovered. "All right, then, here is something you won't be able to resist...a made-to-order pizza. And whatever you want to drink. And fresh garlic bread. *And* dessert—which you'll get to choose. Wow, I'm making myself hungry!''

"We're not bidding on anything," Lauren said sweetly. "We've decided to keep the money instead."

The other contestants gasped.

Bobby Dixon paled. "Surely you don't mean that."

"Yes." Shannen nodded. "We do."

Beside him, Ty heard Reggie Ellis chortle.

"Bobby'll be called on the carpet for this. He was supposed to get all the cash back. Guess nobody thought it was possible for any of them to hold out against all this food after what they haven't been eating. But now there's *two* holding out with a cool grand."

"Guess nobody thought the twins would love the feel of that cash in their little hands so very much," muttered Ty.

Reggie nodded, guffawing. "Think the network will deduct the twins' thousand bucks from Bobby's paycheck?"

Bobby must have thought so, because he went into an auctioneering frenzy, offering every kind of food and drink imaginable to entice the twins to bid. Long after Konrad, Rico and Cortnee had spend every cent of their five hundred dollars and proclaimed themselves stuffed to the point of nausea, Bobby kept it up.

And Shannen and Lauren refused to bid on anything.

"Give it up, Slick B," Konrad said at last. "They ain't buyin' whatever you're sellin'."

"I guess not." Bobby managed a tight-lipped smile. "Color me amazed at the strength of your willpower, girls."

Color me unfazed, Ty thought grimly. He'd already seen Shannen's willpower in action, and Lauren had given him a hint as to how much they wanted money. Given a choice of a thousand dollars between them and a chance to eat, it was no contest at all.

Bobby was visibly displeased. This outcome was obviously not what he and The Powers That Be had intended.

"Okay, listen up, everybody! After bidding and eating all that food, are you ready for a surprise?" Bobby asked robotically, following the script as previously written without noting the twins' unexpected lack of participation.

"This auction is also an immunity contest." Bobby's flat tone failed to convey excitement. "The person with the most money left is the one who wins immunity at the tribal council vote-out tonight."

"Hardly the moment of suspense you were hoping for, huh, Slick Bob?" Rico cackled. "We all know right off the bat who gets immunity. The twins. Too bad they aren't one person."

"Funny, that's what our mother said when we were born," Lauren piped up. "And many many times after."

Shannen gave her sister a censorial nudge that only Ty recorded with his camera. Everybody else was watching Bobby trying to smile deeply enough to get his dimples back in place.

The twins' mother was not entranced with the prospect of twins? Ty pondered that as he studied the sisters' identical looks of chagrin. Both appeared to regret Lauren's impulsive revelation.

"Does this mean both Shannen and Lauren get immunity?" Cortnee asked.

"No!" Bobby was quick to reply. "Only one can have immunity. Shannen and Lauren, one of you gets the totem pole and one of you goes to the meeting tonight without its protection."

"I can almost read your mind, so why don't you go ahead and say it, Bobby?" Shannen challenged him. "One of us goes to the meeting tonight to be voted off, am I right?"

Bobby went into a soliloquy that he'd obviously rehearsed, about one twin facing the prospect of leaving her twin sister on the island. Which one would it be? He gestured to the twins, directorially calling to the cameras to focus on them.

"You girls will have to make the decision yourselves, to choose which one of you gets the immunity totem," Bobby added dramatically.

Ty zeroed in on Shannen. Her expression was priceless, and he came close to laughing out loud.

"Do you expect us to have a catfight or something?" Shannen glowered at Bobby. "Not a chance! Lauren, you take the immunity totem. I'll brave the council on my own."

Shannen waited expectantly for Lauren to make the same offer back to her. She would insist that Lauren keep the totem pole, of course, but she fully expected Lauren to refuse at least once.

"Thanks, Shannen!" Lauren was all smiles as she threw her arms around Shannen's neck. "You're the best sister in the world!"

"I'll say she is!" seconded an admiring Konrad. "Because you know we're going to vote you off tonight, Shannen. Nothing personal, but we can't keep two of you around anymore."

"I understand. Two of a kind is one too many," Shannen murmured.

She managed to smile, though she felt sick with disappointment. It surprised her; she didn't think being out of the game would bother her so much.

Shannen kept her eyes away from Ty and clutched her money, smiling till her face hurt.

She wanted a little time alone with Lauren, but the cameras constantly stayed on them both. Hoping for some sort of sisterly tiff?

It didn't happen. The twins didn't mention the immunity issue. They recounted their hundred-dollar bills, all ten of them.

For a change, Ty wasn't filming them, Shannen noted.

He'd staked out a place on the beach by Konrad and Cortnee.

Cortnee was trying to teach Konrad some dance steps, and they both laughed uproariously at his failed attempts to match hers. Rico lay on the sand, clutching his stomach and groaning about the too-rich meal he'd eaten.

"Do you think Shannen will get voted off tonight?" Heidi asked Ty as they set up for filming at the tribal council area later that night.

"I didn't hear Rico or Cortnee jump in to refute Konrad when he said they'd vote her off, but who knows?" Ty shrugged.

"After experiencing Shannen's PMS moments today, I have to say that I like Lauren better," admitted Heidi. "She's always so sweet."

"PMS moments?" echoed Ty. "I believe Shannen blamed her bout of temper this morning on being accosted by a germ last night."

The germ being him, of course. And he hadn't accosted her! He frowned. Why had he prolonged this stupid conversation with Heidi, anyway? Because he wanted to talk about Shannen at every opportunity with anyone? He was bordering on pathetic!

"A germ is just a euphemism for PMS, of course," scoffed Heidi. "Like I used to call my ex-fiancé a germ because he made me sick."

Now that was definitely a discussion to avoid. Ty pretended to be completely absorbed in adjusting the angle of the standing camera.

The contestants filed into the meeting place, and Bobby launched into a long monologue about the Final Four and Destiny.

Shannen barely tuned in to listen. She was too preoccupied to pay attention and kept looking around, trying to prepare herself for the voting to come.

She knew she was going to be voted off and so did everybody else. She wouldn't throw a tantrum over it as some others had, Shannen vowed. She wouldn't tear up and babble something insipidly sentimental, either. She was going to make a graceful exit, smiling, saying it had been fun and wishing the others good luck.

Reflexively she located Ty behind his camera. He wasn't looking at her; he was filming Cortnee, who was chatting quietly with Konrad while Bobby droned on. It was strange not to have Ty's full attention, not to have him watching her through his lens.

Shannen realized just how accustomed she'd become to having him focus on her. But from the time the auction had ended this afternoon, he had ignored her, filming everyone else *but* her.

She thought back to the passionate kiss Lauren had interrupted this morning. No use kidding herself—that had been a kiss meant to lead to much more. And it was her last private interaction with Tynan and had ended on a sour note, with her snapping at him, glaring as she left him.

But that was how most of their encounters on this island ended, and it had never altered his behavior toward her. Invariably, the next time she saw him, he would be watching her, that intense look in his eye as his camera rolled.

But now…he didn't even glance her way when he thought she might not be looking. She knew because she watched him covertly but constantly.

She felt anxiety begin a slow, steady build inside her. Ty was acting as though he was completely uninterested in her.

Because he was? Shannen fought against the sinking of her heart.

We'll make plans to see each other after the game, to continue what we've begun. To be together. She closed her eyes and could hear his voice as she relived their brief time together this morning at the spring. *I want us to be together, Shannen. I want you to want that, too.*

She felt Lauren's hand squeeze hers.

"Shannen, don't fall asleep during Bobby's big talk," she whispered. "Though it's tempting 'cause he's such a windbag." Lauren giggled.

Shannen opened her eyes. Cameraman Reggie was filming her and Lauren, and Ty still wasn't looking their way. If—when!—she was voted out of the game tonight, she knew she would go to a nearby island to stay with the last seven contestants who'd been voted off the island.

There was a hotel there where they all stayed until it was time for "jury duty," when the ten rejected contestants would appear at the final tribal council to vote for a winner, choosing between the Final Two.

She would be over there, and Ty would be here on this island, filming the surviving contestants all day and spending the nights in the crew's camp. She wouldn't see him anymore!

Shannen inhaled a sharp breath of dismay. Though she'd told Ty repeatedly that she didn't want to see him, that whatever was growing between them was over, at last she faced the truth.

She wanted what Ty had said he wanted. *We'll make plans to see each other after the game, to continue what we've begun. To be together.*

But how could she tell him so, if she were on some other island? She knew the procedure: the rejects gathered their belongings immediately after the vote and were whisked away in a boat, not to be seen again.

The departure was never filmed. A pair of production assistants accompanied the loser until the boat left shore. She wouldn't have the chance to say anything to Ty.

When would she see him again? When the jury of contestants were brought back to the island to cast their votes for the winner? There would be no chance to be alone with Ty then.

The anxiety swirling through her was awful; she hadn't felt this nervous about a man since she'd been back in high school, wondering if Ty would call her.

In the midst of her unbridled emotional storm, the voting came as a distinct anti-climax. Shannen cast her vote against Rico.

"Nothing personal," she said, as the cameraman—who was not Ty—filmed her slipping her vote into the box.

Konrad, Rico and Cortnee voted against Shannen, as she'd expected. No, it wasn't personal, and she didn't take it that way. If she'd kept the immunity totem herself, they would have voted off Lauren. The alliance had included both twins until now, when one had to go.

What surprised her most was Lauren's vote against Cortnee. Was this the second time she'd done so? Ty would think so.

Ty. He was filming Rico, Cortnee and Konrad, who were trying to look somber over Shannen's dismissal and not quite pulling it off. She knew the relief they were feeling at having survived another round. Until tonight she'd felt that same way after each vote.

"Shannen, your light has been extinguished." Bobby took Shannen's flashlight, a symbol of her banishment. A torch would've been more dramatic, but *Victorious* had opted not to be totally derivative.

"It's better this way, Shan," Lauren whispered into her ear. "I'll be able to play Konrad and Rico against Cortnee. I know you wouldn't do it that way, but it's going to work, you'll see. They like me better than Cortnee."

"Ready to go, Shannen?" The two male production assistants, Kevin and Adam, came to Shannen's side.

"Let's get your stuff and put you on the boat," said one.

"You're going to love the hotel," enthused the other.

"It's a first-class resort with all the amenities. You can do anything you want and eat as much as you want. Think of it as a free vacation!"

She knew they were being kind, trying to ease the sting of being voted off. She smiled at them as she slipped an arm through each of theirs. "Thanks, guys."

She cast a final look back. If she were on camera, it would appear that she was taking a last glance at the familiar setting, or maybe checking on her twin.

But she wasn't on camera. Filming had stopped, and the crew was packing up the equipment. Ty chatted with the female production assistants, one of them Heidi.

For the first time, Shannen felt a stab of jealousy at the sight of Ty talking to another woman. He and Heidi would certainly have a lot in common, working in the same industry, on the same show. Did Heidi know his last name was Howe, not Hale? Shannen doubted it. Ty made it clear that his new life—

His new life. *His life without money!* Suddenly all the pieces began to fit, creating the most dismal picture. Shannen wanted to cry out with pain.

Suddenly she understood it all.

Ty's blatant loss of interest in her occurred right after she'd given the immunity totem to Lauren. *The moment it became clear that she wasn't going to win the game and the prize money.*

In fact, she wouldn't win a cent, since she hadn't made it to the Final Four. The auction money she'd held on to wouldn't interest him, not when he'd been hoping to rekindle a flame with the million-dollar winner.

It was weirdly cosmic that Ty, having been plagued by fortune hunters until the fall of the House of Howe, should seek to become a fortune hunter himself.

And now that she had no prospects for a fortune, he had abruptly given her up.

Shannen stoically held back her tears. She hadn't felt this hopeless since she was back in high school and Ty had ended it between them.

The hotel on the island lived up to the PA's promise. It was a first-class resort with all the amenities, including two swimming pools, one indoors and one outdoors connected by a tunnel one swam through, two bars, one small and dark and quiet, one noisy and raucous with a live band and dance floor. There were three dining rooms, each differently themed, and—perhaps to counteract all those gourmet meals—a fully equipped gym and steam room.

An enthusiastic young staffer, Miles, who worked for *Victorious* and was "in charge of the contestants here" gave Shannen the grand tour of the facilities.

"Tonight everybody's in the Parrot Room dancing," said Miles. "By everybody, I mean the contestants and the *Victorious* staff who are assigned here. We all hang out together. It's like one big spring break around here."

She'd arrived in the lowest spirits, but Shannen felt herself respond to the resort's allure. She'd seen places like this on *Lifestyles of the Rich and Famous* but had never expected to set foot in one.

"Seems like you have a better job being stationed here than the crew stuck filming on the island," she remarked.

"My uncle is Clark Garrett," confided Miles. "You'd better believe I decided to stay in this place instead of that bug-ridden crew camp."

He led her to her room and opened the door. "Order anything you want from room service, the network is picking up the tab." Miles was expansive. "And come down to the Parrot Room and join us later. They have a great band."

"Thanks, but I'm tired." Shannen gazed around her room, at the king-size bed, which had already been turned down invitingly.

The clean white sheets and big pillows piled high against

the bamboo headboard beckoned. She glanced at the screen door, opening onto a balcony that held a chaise longue and a round table with two chairs. The ocean breezes wafted through the curtains, filling the room with the cool refreshing scent of the sea.

"This looks like heaven." She sighed. "After I take a shower, I'm going to bed and sleep for the next three days."

Miles laughed. "Everybody says that when they first arrive here. But by tomorrow afternoon, I predict you'll be at the swimming pool and making plans to join us for dinner and dancing." He handed her the room key. "Your bag is in the closet—you remember, the one you packed in case you made it here."

Shannen remembered when she and Lauren had packed their bags according to the show's directive, bringing basics for a short stay at the hotel, should they survive long enough to be among the jury. How excited and nervous they'd been!

Now Lauren had made it to the Final Four and would definitely receive some prize money. Plus, she still had a chance to go all the way and win the million dollars.

That thought put a spring into her step as Shannen said goodbye to Miles. After carefully placing the thousand dollars' auction money in the small room safe, she headed straight for the spacious bathroom, bypassing the whirlpool for the shower stall.

There was plenty of water, soap and shampoo—things she'd taken for granted until she'd been deprived of them during her *Victorious* stint. It was sheer bliss!

After taking the longest shower of her life, she wrapped herself in a thick terry robe monogrammed with the hotel's name and smoothed coconut-scented lotion all over herself. As she dried her hair, she debated whether to go right to bed or to call room service and order something to eat. Could she stay awake that long?

She turned off the dryer and brushed her hair until it hung straight and sleek around her shoulders. After the lack of mirrors on the island, being able to see what she was doing was a luxury in itself.

Shannen heard the knock at the door and padded over to it, expecting to see Miles through the peephole, knowing she was going to turn down any other invitation to join the *Victorious* gang tonight.

Her heart slammed against her ribs, and she took another long look, wondering if she were hallucinating. Because it wasn't the young staffer standing outside in the hallway.

It was Tynan.

The rush of adrenaline that surged through her nearly knocked her off her feet.

He rapped again. "Open up, Shannen. I just heard you turn off the hair dryer, so I know you can hear me."

Shannen opened the door and stared at him, stupefied. "How…how did you—"

"I have my ways. Aren't you going to invite me in?"

She couldn't seem to breathe, let alone speak. Shannen could only gape at him, as if he were an apparition from some astral plane. An apparition wearing the same baggy khaki shorts and white T-shirt with the network's logo imprinted on the front, the clothes that he had worn all day today.

She'd certainly spent enough hours looking at him today to remember his clothing down to the exact detail. Equally unforgettable was the fact that he'd ignored her from the moment it was clear that she was no longer a million-dollar contender.

But now he was here. Shannen folded her arms in front of her chest in classic defense mode, blocking his way.

"Luckily I'm not a vampire, so I don't have to wait for an invite before entering," Ty said lightly and walked into the room.

He stepped around her, but only because she stepped out

of his way. If she hadn't moved, he seemed ready and willing to move her himself.

He looked around the room. "Nice. Bet you're not a bit nostalgic for the crowded old tent back on the island, hmm?"

Shannen finally found her voice. "Since being in the crowded old tent would mean I was still in the running to win the game, I'd rather be there than here. Though they've spared no expense to make us feel less like losers and more like tourists, I guess."

Ty had stooped to open the door of the small refrigerator in the corner of the room. "Plenty of snacks in here. Hawaiian macadamia nuts, cheeses, crackers. Cookies, fruit and yogurt. Miniature bottles of every kind of alcohol you can think of. A few full-size bottles of beer and wine, too."

"Miles would tell you to help yourself, it's on the network's tab," said Shannen, striving for a tone of nonchalance. By the tremor in her voice, she was fairly certain she hadn't pulled it off.

"Who's Miles?" Ty continued to peruse the fridge.

"Clark Garrett's nephew. He stays here and baby-sits us *Victorious* rejects."

"Oh, yes, the nephew." Ty chuckled. "I've heard about him from Heidi and the other PAs. They think he's a fool to be stuck over here while they get the on-location experience with the crew. They're sure his TV career won't last long, uncle or not, but I told them never to underestimate the power of nepotism in the industry."

He stood up, his hands filled with bottles and food packages. "The food isn't up for auction, and you don't have to worry about cheating anymore. Come on out here and enjoy it with a clear conscience, Shannen."

Without waiting for her to reply, he carried the food and drink outside to the balcony and placed them on the table.

Shannen was nonplussed to the point of inaction. Silently she watched Ty settle back on the chaise longue, one leg stretched out, his other foot on the ground. He opened a bottle of beer and took a swallow.

It occurred to her that she was clad only in the hotel robe. "I...have to get dressed," she called weakly, and snatched a bright red-and-yellow-flowered sundress and underwear from her suitcase.

She dressed in the bathroom and, taking a deep breath, joined Ty on the balcony.

"You clean up well." He gave her a slow, thorough appraisal as she stood beside the door.

"Are you going to tell me why you're here, or am I supposed to guess?" Shannen wanted to recall the words the moment she'd uttered them.

"Oh, definitely, go ahead and guess," Ty invited, laughter gleaming in his eyes. "I can't wait to hear what you'll come up with."

"I knew you'd say something like that," muttered Shannen.

"So why am I here, Shannen?"

"I'm too tired to play games," she said tersely, knowing it was a lie. She might've been tired before, but she was wide awake now. Every nerve in her body felt wired. "How did you get here, anyway? And find my room?"

"A couple of network honchos are here to discuss plans for the *Victorious* reunion show. I know, you're probably thinking—the game isn't over and they're already talking about a reunion?" Ty took another swig of the beer. "But our far-thinking executives like to plan ahead. Or more likely, they saw the chance for a company-paid vacation and grabbed it. I volunteered to bring the past few days' footage over for their viewing pleasure."

"So you took the boat here," Shannen concluded.

"As you know, it's a short ride. I was accompanied by Kevin and Adam, who went straight to the Parrot Room. Since I'm officially with the program, all I had to do to get your room number was to ask the desk clerk. Are we finished with the Q and A?''

Shannen concentrated on opening a package of crackers and tried to keep her voice steady. "I'm surprised to see you.''

"I could tell." He leaned forward, his hands resting on his thighs. "What I can't tell is if you're glad or totally indifferent or smoldering with anger. You can be pretty hard to read sometimes, Shannen.''

"As if you're an open book!" Shannen dropped the crackers and headed inside.

"Ah, a clue." Ty followed her into the room. "The answer is C—smoldering with anger. Next question. Are you mad at me or your sister or the other contestants—or just ticked off with life in general?''

She turned to him, startled. "Why would I be mad at Lauren?''

"Maybe because she hung on to that immunity totem pole and didn't even make you a token offer? Which you would've nobly declined, of course.''

It was unnerving that he had voiced exactly what she had thought at the time. A disloyal pang of guilt surged through her.

"I wanted Lauren to have it." Shannen was defensive. "She knew that.''

Ty shrugged. "Sure, but still—it would've been nice if she'd at least made the gesture.''

Shannen saw the glint in his eye. "You're trying to be an instigator!''

"No, a detective. If you won't tell me why you're upset, I'm going to have to figure it out for myself. Unless you're not upset at all…just nervous. Just stalling." It took him only two steps to be standing directly in front of her. "If that's the case, let me assuage your jitters.''

Shannen sucked in a breath. "If you're thinking that because Lauren is still in the game and could win the money—''

''I'm not thinking about Lauren or the game or the money, Shannen.'' He cupped her cheek with his hand.

Reflexively Shannen closed her eyes and leaned into his hand, letting the warmth of his palm envelop her. If she intended to tell him to leave, this was the time to do it, a small voice inside her head counseled.

''How can I think of anything else but you?'' His voice was a low, seductive growl. He curved his other hand over her hip in a firm possessive grasp.

Shannen's eyes stayed closed. She didn't want him to go, she achingly admitted to herself. But...

''Everything is so...unfinished between us, Ty,'' she whispered.

''I think it's time we altered that, don't you?'' Ty nibbled on her earlobe, his voice husky.

He trailed kisses along the curve of her jaw. When his mouth finally, lightly brushed hers, she exhaled with a hushed whimper. Raising her arms slowly, she laid her hands against his chest, feeling his body heat through the well-washed cotton material of his shirt.

It was all the invitation Ty needed to deepen the kiss. He opened his mouth over hers, luring her tongue into an erotic duel with his. Shannen felt desire and urgency erupt inside her with breathtaking speed, as though this morning's interrupted passion had been simmering deep within her, just waiting for the spark to ignite into a full blaze.

Ty sank down onto the edge of the bed, pulling her down on his lap. ''I want you so much, Shannen,'' he groaned, nuzzling her neck while his busy fingers pulled down the long zipper of her sundress.

His fingertips stroked her bare back and she shivered with response. Her sundress had a built-in bra, baring her breasts as it lay open around her waist. Ty caressed the nape of her neck and the smooth line of her shoulders before slipping in front to take possession of her breasts, which were swollen and sensitive with arousal.

Shannen felt lost in a sensual dream. She tangled her fingers in the dark thickness of his hair, holding his head to hers and kissing him hungrily. How many times had she fantasized being alone with him like this? For the past nine years, he'd been her fantasy lover.

And now, at last…

All rational thought fled, taking her self-control along with it. Shannen was only too willing to cede command to the voluptuous emotions surging through her body.

Ty lay back on the bed, his arms tightly around her, taking her with him. Her dress tangled around her legs, and he pulled it off in one deft sweep, tossing it to the floor. He eased her onto her back, his eyes dark and intense, drinking in the sight of her.

Instead of the self-consciousness she might've expected under such careful scrutiny, Shannen basked in the heat of his admiring stare.

"I need you, Shannen. I've wanted you for so long," he murmured hoarsely.

She lifted her hand and traced the fine shape of his mouth, her voice throaty with enticement and challenge.

"Show me, Tynan."

Seven

The need to feel his skin against hers was overpowering. Shannen slid her hands under his shirt and tugged at it. Responding to her demand, he yanked the T-shirt off, giving her access to the smooth, muscled expanse of his torso. Her hands and lips roamed his chest, feeling every smooth inch of his skin and the contrasting wiry hair.

He was equally thorough with her, learning the shape of her breasts with his hands, tasting the taut buds with his lips. At long last one of his hands traveled lower, pausing to trace her navel, to caress the pale hollow of her stomach. He found her center, his slow sultry strokes into her liquid heat rendering her mindless with pleasure.

The rest of their clothing was shed with mutual haste and sent flying in different directions. They kissed again and again, their kisses deep and passionate and growing more urgent.

Shannen clung to Ty, drunk on the taste and the smell and the feel of him. He touched her intimately again and she moaned, arching to him. Blindly, she scored her fingernails along his belly, to wrap her hand around the hard pulsing length of his arousal.

Their eyes met.

"I bought condoms at the shop here in the hotel," Ty said bluntly. "They're in the pocket of my shorts somewhere on the floor."

"You bought them before you came to my room tonight?" Shannen felt herself blushing, not sure what embarrassed her more—his frankness or his confidence. "You were that sure of me?"

It was his confidence, she decided. And it didn't embarrass her as much as irritate her. Immensely.

She sat up, averting her eyes from the sight of Ty retrieving the foil packets from the pocket of his khaki shorts.

"Let's just say I was hopeful." His ardor was undiminished by this break in their foreplay and appeared likewise immune from accusation in her voice.

She knew because she kept stealing glances at him, in spite of her resolve not to. "Do you think I'm that easy?" she snapped. "So easy that all you have to do is to show up at my door and I'll go to bed with you?"

It didn't help that she'd proved that statement to be true. The self-incrimination increased her agitation.

"Shannen, one thing you definitely are not is easy," Ty said, his tone heartfelt.

A bit too heartfelt. Her brows narrowed. "What do you mean by that?"

"It's taken us nine years to get to this point, which is so far beyond easy that—"

"Don't try to tell me you've been pining for me for the past nine years, because I won't believe you, Tynan." Shannen grabbed the edge of the quilt comforter and pulled it over her, covering herself. "And…and don't give me that oh-so-noble 'you were too young' speech again."

"You told me this afternoon that you understood, Shannen." Ty groaned. "But if you're determined to hold a grudge because I couldn't take advantage of—"

"I turned twenty-one five years ago, Ty," Shannen said crossly. "Legal age. But you didn't bother to look me up then. No, you forgot all about me until you saw me on this island."

And realized I had a chance to win a million dollars, she added to herself. No use bringing that up now, when she was out of the running.

"I know when you turned twenty-one, Shannen. It was two years after the Howes had spent months on the front pages of every paper in the country and became joke fodder for comedians, morality sermons for the clergy and all the rest that goes with being a notorious media staple. I truly didn't think you would welcome a national pariah on your doorstep."

"All of that was about the other Howes. *You* didn't do anything wrong. At least do me the favor of being honest with me, Tynan. Admit that you never once considered coming back to West Falls to see me."

"I did, Shannen."

"Of course you'd say that *now!* You're wearing a condom—and…and keeping it on while I'm yelling at you!"

His lips quirked. "Not as difficult as it seems since you're naked in bed and I want you more than I've ever wanted a woman in my life, Shannen."

"Which proves my point. You'd say anything to—"

"I want to make love with you, Shannen. I've been honest about it, I haven't tried to trick you into anything." He sat down on the bed and carefully lifted the quilt from her. "You want me, too. We aren't playing a game of easy or hard to get. And thanks to tonight's vote, we're free from the *Victorious* game, too."

He leaned over her, and as his head descended, Shannen was fully aware of what was coming next. And welcomed it, she allowed herself to admit. She was weary of putting up roadblocks between them. This wasn't a game. This was Tynan, whom she'd longed for since she was seventeen.

Never mind that in her girlish daydreams they had been in love when they made love. She was all grown up now; she knew lovemaking didn't have to include true love.

A small wistful sigh escaped from her throat as his mouth touched hers. Being with Ty tonight would be enough. It would have to be enough.

She held him tight as he gently yet inexorably pressed into her.

"Sweetheart," he whispered hoarsely, dropping his head to her breast. He had stopped moving, allowing her body time to adjust before fully sheathing himself in her liquid heat.

Shannen caressed him, her hands gliding over the full length of his back from his shoulders to his hips, savoring the feel of him in her arms, in her body. Her fingers tightened around him, pressing him down as she arched her hips upward, inching him even deeper inside her.

"More, Ty." She pressed again.

He resisted. "Shannen, you're so small, so tight. Let's take it slowly. I don't want to hurt you."

She shook her head. "You won't, you can't. I want all of you inside me now, Ty. I'm tired of waiting. We've already waited too long."

"Way too long," he agreed fervently. He filled her with one long thrust, then began to move, teasing her by withdrawing almost completely, waiting for her to moan his name before moving forward again.

He kept up the slow steady rhythm until she squirmed beneath him, locking her limbs around him in a silent plea. Ty wasn't one to settle for silence.

"Tell me what you want." He chuckled softly. "Faster, like this?" He moved faster, just as she wanted him to and then stopped, as if awaiting further instructions.

"Deeper?" he suggested, proceeding while she gasped

with pleasure. He stopped to propose, "Harder?" and to demonstrate exactly how that felt, too.

Shannen's breath caught. His teasing was sexy and arousing and maddening, all at the same time. "Yes," she panted. "Faster, deeper, harder. Please, oh, please!"

Every sensual nerve ending had caught fire and burned as their movements created a blaze that threatened to consume her. No, not *threaten,* she dizzily corrected. There was nothing threatening about this union with Ty.

Promise was the correct description. Their sexual conflagration promised to consume her and she wanted that—she wanted all barriers between them melted away forever.

And they were. The wild, intense pleasure finally overwhelmed them at the same moment. Shannen cried his name as she shattered into a thousand pieces. Through the firestorm she heard Ty call out for her as he pulsed inside her, their essences joined as they became truly one.

She was only vaguely aware of his weight collapsing upon her. It was the heat of his body covering her that penetrated her sensuous daze. It complemented the inner warmth that filled her with a sense of utter completeness.

Slowly she resurfaced, opening her eyes to find him smiling down at her. Their bodies were still joined, and she had no intention of moving. He stirred above her, but she tightened her legs and arms around him.

"Don't move." She purred the command into his ear.

"I'm too heavy for you," he protested, but he didn't move away from her. He trailed a string of gossamer-light kisses along her neck, licking and nipping her skin. "I can't get enough of you, Shannen."

His hands found hers, his fingers intertwining with hers. He felt satiated; he felt a kind of peace he'd never known. This sweet, languid time—with Shannen in his arms, defenseless and utterly trusting, no walls or barriers between them—was like nothing he'd ever known.

He raised his head and smiled into her eyes. "I'm trying

to come up with something profound to say that doesn't sound like a cheesy line,'' he admitted quietly. ''Because being with you...''

His voice trailed off. There really were no words to describe how he was feeling right now.

I love you sprang to mind, and he dismissed it just as quickly. No, that was beyond cheesy, it was more like fraud. According to the Book of Howe, love had nothing to do with what he felt for Shannen right now. It was the pleasurable afterglow of sex.

But to say *that* would be tactless—and then some.

''I'd love to know what you're really thinking.'' Shannen was staring deeply into his eyes. ''Your expression keeps changing, like there's a civil war going on in your head.''

''An astute observation.'' Ty slowly disengaged his body from hers and sat up. She was scarily close to the mark. He drew her into the circle of his arms and leaned back against the pillows.

''I'd like to know what *you're* really thinking, Shannen.'' He brushed his lips lightly over her hair, the clean, fresh scent of coconut shampoo filling his nostrils.

He wasn't simply trying to divert her from gaining access to his own conflicted thoughts, he assured himself; he was genuinely interested in her take on this development in their ever-evolving relationship.

''I already told you.'' She cast him a glance beneath her lashes. ''That I'd love to know what you're really thinking.''

''A winning combination of flirtatious and evasive.'' He was glad she was playing it this way, Ty decided. Keeping it light instead of getting all carried away with deep talk of love and promises.

Shannen studied him and had no trouble reading the relief that crossed his face. It was fortunate that she'd snuffed her afterglow impulse to rhapsodize about their love-making.

She wanted to tell him that being with him not only lived up to her long-held fantasies but exceeded them, that she not only loved having sex with him, she loved *him,* Ty Hale, the ex-Howe who worked for a living.

She supposed she could've at least told him that she'd never known making love could be this way, that with him she'd had her very first climax, but then he might feel encouraged to share his sexual history with her. Which she didn't want to hear.

Nor did she care to go into detail about her own lack of experience, which consisted only of Ben Salton, her college boyfriend and first lover. She'd been Ben's first lover, too, and their fumbling clumsy sex had been so awkward and miserable for them both that a year after they'd broken up and Ben had found someone new, he'd actually called Shannen to tell her that sex could be good, not awful, and she shouldn't let their unskilled forays keep her from trying it again—with someone else, of course.

Shannen had thanked good old Ben and wished him luck with his new love but declined to venture back into the sexual arena. From what she could tell, there were too many negatives and not a single positive, especially since she'd firmly suppressed any hopes of ever being with Tynan Howe. He was a closed chapter in her life.

Which had been now reopened.

Or had it?

That she had satisfied him, Shannen had no doubt, but he'd made a point of holding back the words that would elevate tonight from hot one-night stand to something more.

Something involving love and trust and commitment.

So she would follow his lead. No opening her heart to him, the way she had as a naive schoolgirl in love. He'd *crushed* her back then, and it wasn't going to happen again. She was a gameworthy opponent now.

A loud and unexpected knock sounded at the door, jolting them both from the thoughtful silence enshrouding them.

"Probably a maid," said Ty. "Tell her to—"

"Lauren, baby, are you still awake?" an urgent male voice called from the hall. "Lauren, open up. It's Jed."

Shannen sprang from the bed, her actions sheer reflex. *Jed?* she mouthed to Ty, who looked as startled as she did.

"He thinks I'm Lauren," she said in a whisper. "He called her 'baby'!"

"Lauren, come on! Let me in!" Jed's voice rose, the words slurring.

"Do you think he's been drinking?" whispered Shannen, still trying to process Jed's appearance at what he thought was Lauren's hotel room door—and demanding to be let in!

"I'd count on it," Ty muttered back. "Tell him to get lost, Shannen."

"Why would he think I'm Lauren?" She still looked confused.

"I'm going to hazard a guess. The resort has no TV access, and even if it did, nobody would know you'd been voted off the island yet. Someone would've had to tell the *Victorious* jury pool down in the Parrot Room which contestant arrived at the hotel tonight."

"And somebody said it was a twin and Jed assumed it was Lauren?" Shannen surmised with a scowl. "Why would he assume that my sister would get voted off before me?"

"Just making a guess here." Ty made a sound halfway between a groan and a chuckle. "But I think Kevin and Adam, the PAs who came to the hotel with me tonight, told Jed that Lauren was here."

"Lauren!" Jed was pounding on the door now. "Baby!"

"Kevin and Adam know that Cortnee told Lauren—and everybody else on the island the other day—that Jed had slept with Keri and Lucy,'' Ty continued. ''And since the crew thinks Lauren has a, um, thing for Jed—''

''She does not!'' protested Shannen.

''Whether she does or doesn't, I'm betting those merry pranksters decided to see what would happen when they sent Mr. Adventure Guide to *your* door.''

''Jed couldn't have used my sister. I'd have known somehow, I know I would. But that 'baby' garbage of his is making me sick.'' Shannen was seething. ''He has the unmitigated gall to think that Lauren would let him into her room and—''

''He seems *convinced* Lauren would let him in,'' Ty amended. ''Otherwise, he wouldn't have come up here in the first place, would he?''

''I'm going to find out right now. Jed!'' Her voice went velvety smooth, the anger magically disappearing from her tone but not from her glittering blue eyes. ''Give me a minute. I have to get dressed.''

''No need for that, babe,'' Jed called back.

A murderous expression crossed her face. Shannen whipped on her dress.

''Shannen, no! Whatever you're thinking of doing, don't do it.'' Ty pulled on his khaki shorts and T-shirt, dressing as swiftly as Shannen.

''Hide,'' Shannen ordered. ''In the closet or the shower. Or out on the balcony. I'll close the curtains so he can't see you out there.''

''Hide?'' Ty was appalled. ''You're joking, right?''

''No. I'm going to have a little talk with Jed and—''

''You don't want any witnesses?'' Ty grimaced. ''As for me hiding, forget it. I am not going to hide anywhere. People only do that in soap operas or wacky sitcoms. We're doing a reality show here.''

''This is not any show at all, it's our life,'' Shannen said darkly. ''And if Jed, that lawsuit-happy creep, sees you here, you could very well find yourself getting sued by him.

Or even fired by Clark Garrett for getting sued. You can't lose your job, Ty. You're no longer rich, remember? You work for a living, and take it from someone who always has, that means staying employed. Now, hide!''

She gave him a push toward the balcony and stalked to the door to the hall, flinging it open.

''Hello, Jed.''

''Hi, baby.'' A tousled, wrinkled Jed leaned against the doorjamb. ''Surprised to see me?''

''More than you'll ever know.'' Shannen extended her arm. ''Come in.''

''Oh, yeah, babe.'' Jed ambled into the room. ''Let's just—''

There was a loud rattle, and the door to the balcony was opened and shut with a bang. Shannen and Jed simultaneously turned to see Ty rushing toward them.

''Thank God I made it in time.'' Ty pretended to pant, as if he were out of breath from running and catapulting onto the balcony and bursting into the room. ''The guys told me what they'd done. Jed, this isn't Lauren, it's Shannen, and she isn't very pleased with what's been going on.''

Jed's jaw dropped. His eyes flew to Shannen's face, which was a mask of sheer rage. ''Ah, man!'' he gasped, and headed for the door.

''You're not going anywhere until you tell me why you came skulking up here looking for my sister!'' Shannen caught a handful of Jed's shirt.

He was drunk and off guard and she was pumped with rage, which rendered her surprisingly strong. She gave his shirt a forceful pull, and he stumbled and hit his head on the door frame.

''Ow! You hit me! I didn't do anything wrong!'' Jed wailed. ''Your sister said she—''

''I didn't hit you, you tripped, you clod! And don't you dare say my sister's name!'' Shannen grabbed the knob and swung it back, almost clipping him with it.

"He didn't say it, Shannen," Ty pointed out calmly. Swiftly, he caught her around the waist with one arm and pried her hand from the knob.

"You'd better get out of here now," he warned Jed. "Can't you tell just by looking at her that she has homicide in her heart?"

"I-I'm going. I'm gone!" Jed ran down the hall, disappearing from sight as he turned a corner.

Shannen was so furious, she kicked the door shut. "That jerk, that creep, that—"

"Calm down," ordered Ty, "or else I'll put you in the shower and turn on the cold water. That'll cool you off."

"Oh, just try it!" cried Shannen. "I dare you to try it."

Her eyes were flashing, her face flushed with fury. Ty started to laugh; he couldn't help himself. "You're a fierce one, Shannen. No wonder Jed ran out of here like a spooked horse. You scared him silly."

"You did your part, pretending to crash onto the balcony like…like Zorro. And telling him I had 'homicide in my heart'? Where did that come from?" Shannen gulped back a giggle. Her anger was fast morphing into pure giddiness.

"It was a line from one of the soaps I worked on. I stored it away for future use, but this was the first time I ever thought it might apply." A slow grin crossed Ty's face. "It's a line that requires a certain kind of overblown situation like, uh, this one."

"It's true, scenes like this don't come along every day," agreed Shannen.

"For that, we can only be thankful," Ty said dryly.

Shannen smiled with satisfaction. "I really did scare the rat, didn't I?"

"You scared him." There was a teasing glint in Ty's dark eyes. "I'm curious as to what you planned to do with him, though."

She shrugged. "I didn't have any real plan—I thought I'd improvise as I went along. I just wanted him to know he'd made a major mistake trying to...to seduce my sister, and to make sure he wouldn't try it again.''

"Shannen, what if Jed had every reason to believe that Lauren would welcome him?"

"I just don't believe that, Tynan. Obviously, Jed thinks he's irresistible, and after a few drinks he decided to try his charm on my sister, the newcomer to the hotel. Except he had the bad luck of finding me here instead.''

"He'd probably agree with you on the bad luck part, Shannen. But keep in mind, you had the element of surprise going for you at first. It wouldn't have been long before he recovered himself, and even with him drunk, you would've been in big trouble.''

"I guess so. I know how strong he is from all those stupid contests.''

"I'd like to hear you admit that my appearance was most timely, Shannen. Even if my entrance was...shall we say Zorroesque?'' Ty wrapped her in his arms.

"I admit it. Your appearance was most timely, Tynan.'' She put her arms around him and leaned into him. "And if you'd rather, I could liken it to Batman instead of Zorro.''

"You're still not taking the risk seriously, and I can't stand the thought of you getting hurt. If Jed had tried, I would've—'' Ty paused, considering.

"Beaten him up?'' Shannen suggested, cuddling closer. "You're so strong, you could take him easily.''

"Appealing to my inner Neanderthal?'' He kissed the top of her head. "I didn't know I had one until tonight.''

They stood together for a few quiet moments, holding each other as the tension from the encounter with Jed drained away. And then, a distinct rumble came from the vicinity of her abdomen.

Her stomach was growling! "Ohhhh!'' Embarrassed, Shannen tried to draw back. "Sorry.''

Ty held her firm. "Nothing to be sorry about. When was

the last time you had a decent meal, anyway? Call room service right now and order something.''

''On the network's tab,'' they chorused together, laughing.

''I know exactly what I want.'' She headed for the phone beside the bed. ''A turkey sandwich with cheese, lettuce and tomato with honey mustard. I've been dying for one of those.''

The food arrived shortly after she called, and Shannen carried it to the table on the balcony. Ty joined her out there while she ate.

''Did I tell you how much I admire your ethics in turning down the food that night on the beach?'' he asked, watching her enjoy every bite of the sandwich.

''Sort of. You sounded more like you were questioning my sanity than admiring my ethics, though,'' she teased.

He shook his head. ''No, I was awestruck. I truly admire your sense of fair play and your willpower, too, Shannen. Keep in mind that I come from a family that's severely deficient in both those qualities.''

''But those qualities aren't deficient in you, Ty,'' Shannen said softly. ''Every family has somebody who's deficient in something. It doesn't mean the whole gene pool is tainted. You have to give yourself a break. You're different from…the others,'' she summarized, because to individually cite his father, brother, sister, cousin and uncle seemed rather excessive.

Ty said nothing.

''I can tell by your expression that you don't think I understand what you've faced, but I do, Ty. I have. In a less public way, of course.'' Shannen finished her sandwich and sipped her iced tea. ''When you called me white trash—''

''Shannen, please believe me when I tell you that I didn't mean it. They were just words I used to drive you away from me because I had to make sure you'd go." Ty was emphatic.

"They were words that hit home because there was truth in them," Shannen continued calmly. "My mother was a wild teen herself and had my older brother, Evan, when she was just sixteen. His father was ten years older than she was, and they'd kept their relationship a secret. When you said what you did, it made me face that I was on the verge of repeating her mistakes. My grandmother had tried so hard to keep my sisters and me from turning out like Mom, and there I was, headed down the same road, anyway."

"I didn't know, Shannen. If I had—"

"You would've found some other words to drive me away?" she suggested with a ghost of a smile. "They probably wouldn't have been as effective. I'd seen how my mother had messed up her life—she's still doing it—and what you said was exactly what I needed to knock some sense into me, as Gramma would say."

"Your grandmother has a lot to say," said Ty, covering her hand with his.

"She raised our sister, Jordan, and Lauren and me. My mother married our father—he was her age and in the army—and had Jordan when they were both just twenty-one. Thirteen months later Lauren and I were born. Obviously, she wasn't thrilled to have twins at that time. Or at any time, really."

Ty winced. "It's too bad she kept telling you so. How did you end up being raised by your grandmother?"

"When Lauren and I were three, our dad was killed in a military training accident and Mom brought us back to West Falls to live with Gramma. Our brother bounced between us and his father. Mom came and went as she pleased."

Shannen paused, thinking back on that less-than-idyllic time. "Poor Gramma! She'd worked hard her whole life running the diner and raising a family, and then we descended on her and stayed till we were all grown up. How someone like Mom and someone like Gramma can be mother and daughter is a mystery, but then I wonder how Mom and my sisters and I can be…'' Her voice trailed off.

"Seems like your mother is the 'mystery.' There are a number of those in the Howe family, too.'' Ty laced his fingers with hers.

"Mom's been married three times and has had so many boyfriends not even *she* can remember them all. She goes to bars and gets drunk and into fights. She's written bad checks and shoplifted and has been in and out of jail. Evan is exactly like her. Gramma ended up using the money saved for improvements to the diner to bail Mom and Evan out of jail.''

"So that's why you and Lauren decided to try out for *Victorious?* For the prize money?'' He appraised her thoughtfully. "I never did believe your cast bio claiming you tried out for the show as a lark.''

"I don't do anything for a lark,'' Shannen said flatly. "I didn't even use those words—the show's publicist came up with them. She said it sounded 'more fun' than admitting we were in the game strictly to win money.''

"The truth is rarely fun for media spinners.''

"But needing money is the only reason why we tried to *win* once we were in the game. If we hadn't thought it was our best shot at staying on the island, we never would've forged an alliance with Jed and Keri and Lucy, who we didn't like from the beginning. Or with Konrad, who made us kind of uneasy.''

"I think you can drop the 'we' and use 'I,' Shannen. Lauren's feelings toward Jed, at least, are different from yours,'' Ty reminded her.

"That's only crew gossip,'' she reminded him.

"Oh, yeah? Then what do you call his arrival at what he thought was Lauren's door tonight? And him calling her baby and—''

"That was all Jed's gargantuan ego." Shannen shuddered. "What would Lauren—or Lucy or Keri for that matter—see in a jerk like Jed?"

"Aside from his boyish good looks? And what about his brawny biceps and polished pecs and the rest of his manly physique? Don't forget his adventure-guide résumé, either. Just quoting from the Internet discussion boards, Shannen," Ty added, laughing at her expression of disgust.

"Oh, ugh! As if he isn't already vain enough!"

"He's also already rich enough not to need the million-dollar prize money," Ty remarked, watching her. "Remember him mentioning his family's winter and summer vacation homes, his beloved silver Lexus and all the other things? You asked what a woman would see in Jed—well, at the very least, there is his money. Wealth can make even a toad appealing."

"You know, you're actually lucky you lost all your money, Ty," Shannen said bluntly. "Because having it made you doubt your own appeal."

"It's not uncommon to wonder if you're valued for yourself or your fortune, Shannen."

"Jed obviously doesn't have such doubts," retorted Shannen. "And now that you're desperate for money like most of us in the world, you're free to feel valued for yourself. Lucky man!"

"Are you so very desperate for money, Shannen?" he probed.

"Not sell-an-organ desperate, but our family definitely can use some extra cash. The bank wouldn't give Gramma as big a loan as she needs for the diner, and her house needs work, too. Major structural stuff. Plus our sister, Jordan, is married to Josh, and they have two little kids. Josh is a really nice guy who's been trying to start his own landscaping business but can't get enough money together to buy the necessary equipment. The bank won't give them a loan, either. Jordan buys powerball lottery tickets, but you know the odds of winning that.''

''About the same as being chosen as a contestant on a show like *Victorious,*'' Ty said wryly. ''But you tried out for it, anyway.''

Shannen rolled her eyes. ''Lauren was the one who wanted to try out. She's been bored in West Falls lately and said she just had to do something different for a change. She begged me to come with her. I went along mainly because I thought we didn't have a chance.''

''You were just humoring her, hmm?''

''I never dreamed we'd be chosen,'' Shannen said with feeling.

''Sweetie, you underestimate *your* appeal.''

''We were only picked because we're twins. I didn't think the producers would go for that gimmick, although Gramma said she wasn't surprised.''

''It seems that Gramma is savvy in the ways of network shows. Beautiful identical twin sisters are—''

''No more quotes from the Internet discussion boards!'' Shannen ordered with mock severity. ''Wouldn't the rumormongers have a field day if word ever got out about us? They'd claim it was a fix. Who would ever believe it was strictly coincidence that I came to the island, and there you were behind the camera?''

''What were those odds?'' murmured Ty.

''Sometimes the odds are incredibly odd. I'll be sure to tell Jordan to keep buying those powerball tickets.'' Shannen drew back, suddenly aware of how long she'd been talking, of how much she'd revealed.

She gave a self-conscious laugh. ''Now, why was I boring you with the history of the Cullens? Oh yes, so you wouldn't feel like the only one out here on this balcony whose family wasn't filled with paragons.''

''You're incapable of boring me, Shannen. You were being kind to me, wage slave though I may be.'' His voice held a challenging note that Shannen immediately mistook for something else.

"I like you better without all your money issues, Ty." She slipped from her chair onto his lap. "That fortune-hunter paranoia of yours was beginning to rub off on me. For a while today I thought you were pretending to be interested in me because I had a chance to win the million-dollar prize."

"What?" His arms clamped around her. "Is that the nonsense you were spouting when I first arrived here? I vaguely remember you saying something about the game and the money. Where did you come up with such a hare-brained idea?"

Beneath her, she could feel the flexing of his muscles as he held her. The warmth of his body heat began to penetrate her.

"After I gave the immunity totem to Lauren and it was clear I was going to be kicked out of the game, you stopped filming me. For the first time since we arrived on the island," she added softly.

"You thought my plans of helping myself to your prize money were finished, so I could stop *pretending* to be interested in you?" Ty was incredulous. He throbbed hard and insistent against her, and he took her hand and placed it against himself. "Does that feel like pretense to you, Shannen?"

"No." Shannen gazed into his eyes.

The sound of his low voice was as intoxicating as his masculine strength. Her breasts were crushed against his chest, and the sensual pressure felt so good.

"Are you still wondering why I turned my camera on the others?" He brushed his lips against hers.

When his tongue flicked to trace the fullness of her lower lip, she quivered. Her head was spinning too much to wonder about anything except the wonder of this moment they shared.

"You were disappointed with your sister and trying hard not to show it." He nibbled at her lips, between words. "It wasn't obvious, but I knew. I hated seeing you in pain, Shannen. I sure as hell didn't want to film it."

"A cameraman giving me some privacy from the camera," whispered Shannen. She kissed his cheek. "Thank you, Ty."

He glided his hands along the length of her spine until he reached her bottom. Provocatively, he traced the line of her panties beneath the silky material of her dress, then kneaded the rounded softness with his strong fingers.

"I want you again, Shannen."

"Yes, Ty." A fast-flowing torrent of desire swept her. The heat of it made her go weak and soft. She couldn't do anything but cling to Ty, to meet and match his demands, kiss for kiss, caress for caress.

He gave a low growl as he slid his hand under her skirt. Her breath caught on a moan as sensual currents eddied through her. His body was taut under her hands, and their mingled murmurs and sighs of passion joined the night sounds in the air.

A burgeoning ache radiated from the tips of her breasts to the liquid heat pooling between her thighs.

"Right here. Right now, Shannen," he demanded huskily.

In one of those sudden moves he executed so well, he scooped her up and carried her to the chaise longue a few feet away.

He came down on top of her, his legs between hers, opening her thighs wider as he settled himself against her. The weight of his body pressed her deeper into the soft cushion of the chaise. Acute pleasure shot through her, and instinctively she thrust her hips in counterpoint.

"That's it, baby!" he groaned. He shifted a little to push up her skirt.

All at once, Shannen felt as if she'd been catapulted out

of a sensuous dream. She tried to sit up but only managed to raise herself a little, using her arms as leverage. "Ty, stop."

He froze. "What's wrong, sweetheart?"

"You called me 'baby.'" Shannen stared up at him.

Ty groaned. "Did you hate it?"

She raised her brows. "I haven't decided. I'll let you know. Meanwhile we have to go inside."

"To bed." Ty sounded hopeful. He slowly eased himself off her and rose to stand. He extended his hand, and she placed hers in his. "You're right, of course." He pulled her to her feet. "The bed is much more comfortable than being out here."

"Out here was fine," she assured him dryly. "It's just that all of a sudden I felt like I'd been shot in the head."

He draped an arm around her and walked her inside the room. "Remind me *never* to call you baby again."

"It was a good thing you did, because it conjured up— well, a baby. A cute little consequence I don't think either of us is ready for at this point." Shannen handed him a foil packet. "We didn't have this with us out there."

A visibly startled Ty gaped at the sight of the condom she'd placed in his hand. "I can't believe I forgot."

"No harm done." Her voice became soft and sultry. "Shall we carry on?"

"I completely forgot." Ty was astounded. "That's never happened before. Not ever, Shannen! You go to my head like a double shot of old Granddaddy's 110 proof whiskey."

"Thank you." Shannen felt pleased with herself. It was thrilling to know that Ty had wanted her so much she'd affected his thought processes. He'd certainly obliterated hers! "Maybe you aren't as vigilant without your fortune to guard," she added thoughtfully.

"Believe me, you can take full credit for blowing my mind. Baby."

They both laughed, a bit uncertainly.

Shannen watched as he tore open the packet and sheathed himself.

His mouth took hers with breathtaking impact, and their interrupted passion instantly flared to flashpoint. Neither could wait. They fell to the bed, her body pliant and supple beneath him. She loved being filled by him and sighed her pleasure.

As they joined together, her body moved with him and for him, exerting sensual demands of her own. Abruptly a tidal wave of ecstasy carried them both to the heights of rapture that went on and on until they both lay sated and spent in each other's arms.

Time seemed to stop. Neither felt the need to move or speak or even think. They lay together, languorous and drowsy, their bodies still joined.

Ty was the first to break the idyllic silence. "I'm falling asleep," he murmured.

"That's okay." She stroked him lovingly, her eyes closed. "So am I."

"Good." He carefully withdrew himself from her and reached down to pull the top sheet over her.

Shannen turned to snuggle close to him again, but he wasn't there. Her eyes flew open.

He had gotten out of bed and was standing beside it. "I have to go."

She watched him hastily pull on his clothes. It occurred to her that this was the second time she'd seen him get dressed tonight, and he was donning his clothes this time as speedily as he had when Jed was caterwauling outside the door. She frowned, not liking the similarity.

Now fully dressed, Ty looked down at her. She looked away, holding the sheet to her chin, suddenly grateful for its protection against his gaze.

Ty heaved a sigh. "Shannen, as much as I want to stay with you, I have to round up the PAs and get back to the

island. Filming starts at dawn, as usual." His lips curved
into a smile. "I'll miss not seeing you stagger out of the
tent first thing in the morning."

Shannen wished he would say that he'd miss *her*. Period.
But she didn't tell him so. She'd already done too much
talking tonight. Now he was ready to leave...because he'd
gotten what he came for?

If it was her total capitulation and surrender to him, the
answer was yes, she mocked herself. And now he was leaving her. She steeled herself against the hurt tearing through
her. She was being unreasonable, and she knew it. Of
course he had to go back to the island.

Anyway, what had she expected from him, a pledge of
true love?

"Good night, Shannen."

Their eyes met and held, and she could do nothing but
gaze at him as his mouth lowered to hers. His lips touched
hers, and her lips parted reflexively in response. The doubt
and anxiety that gripped her for the past few moments dis-
solved as he kissed her deeply.

She responded passionately, feeling the hard heat of him,
physical proof that he wanted her as much as she wanted
him. At least there could be no anxious doubts about that.

Then Ty lifted his lips and cupped her face with his big
hands, staring down at her flushed cheeks and kiss-swollen
lips. "If I don't leave now..."

He shook his head and straightened.

Shannen watched him walk toward the door and vowed
not to ask that Dreadfully Desperate Question: When will
I see you again?

"Don't forget your condoms," she called after him,
clutching the sheet even tighter. She'd meant to sound play-
ful, and surprised herself with her baiting tone.

Ty stopped in his tracks.

Shannen was mortified. How unsubtle could she be! She

may as well have gone ahead and asked him the Dreadfully Desperate Question itself. She didn't dare look at Ty.

"I thought I'd leave them here."

She didn't have to look at him—the droll note in his voice gave her a clear enough picture.

So he found her insecurities amusing? Shannen glowered. "Don't bother. I won't be needing them."

"Yes, you will. Tomorrow night when I come over," he added, quietly closing the door behind him as he left the room.

Eight

It's like one big spring break around here. Miles, the show's production assistant stationed at the hotel, had jovially proclaimed last night.

His words rang in Shannen's head as she stood beside the lagoon-like pool, watching the *Victorious* losers swimming and sunning themselves and consuming tray after tray of brilliant-colored exotic drinks.

During her four years at West Falls University, she had never experienced the fun-in-the-sun revelry of spring break. There hadn't been enough money. Time off from class meant extra time to work for pay.

So shouldn't she join the others and indulge herself in this belated, all-expenses-paid spring break? Instead Shannen sank listlessly onto a cushioned lounge chair.

She was bored. *Bored!* What was the matter with her? Who could be bored in a free tropical paradise?

She could. She was.

All she could think about was Ty. Instead of enjoying

the indoor-outdoor pool with its water slide and tunnel maze, she was sitting here daydreaming about him. She pictured his dark eyes, alternately cool and intense, depending on his mood. Of the passion glittering in them as he looked into her eyes while poised to enter her.

Her pulse began to race, and she tried to banish the provocative images from her mind. But how could she succeed when her body still bore the traces of last night's passionate lovemaking? She was hypersensitive in certain intimate places, tender and achy in others.

And she was all too certain that only Tynan's touch could soothe her—by arousing and satisfying her all over again. And again.

Her whole body flushed. Shannen snatched a drink menu from the table and began to fan herself with it. If merely thinking of him had this effect on her, how would she react to his presence?

And when, exactly, would that be? Would he come to her room tonight? And if he did, what then? He would expect to go to bed with her, and heaven help her, she badly wanted that, too. But after that…

He would head back to the island to film the contestants and she would spend another endless day like this one. Wanting him while wondering what, apart from their sexual chemistry, she meant to him. Waiting for him to say things he may never say.

"Hey, there, you! I'm not sure which one you are, but I remember you said you didn't like to be called 'Twin.'"

Shannen looked up at the sound of the friendly enough voice. She tried not to groan at the sight of Lucy, one of the girls who'd been in her tribe from the beginning of the game, until her recent rejection from the island.

According to Cortnee, Lucy was also one of the girls who'd slept with Jed in hopes of winning his alliance.

"It's Shannen," she supplied her name, hoping she

sounded friendly enough. But not feeling very friendly at all.

"Mind if I sit down?" Lucy dropped into the chair beside Shannen's without waiting for an answer. She was carrying a blue drink in a huge glass shaped like a hurricane lamp. Her words were slurred, her movements awkward, no doubt from the effects of that neutron-blue liquid.

"I want you to know I don't hold it against you for voting me off," Lucy announced.

"Thanks," murmured Shannen. "I guess we all have to go sometime—except for the winner, of course."

"The winner," repeated Lucy. "Wonder who that's gonna be?"

"I don't know. I wish it would be my sister."

"Oh, yeah, the other twin." Lucy took a long gulp of her drink. "Hey, are you the one Jed's been messing around with?" She looked confused. "Or is it that other one?"

"It's neither of us," Shannen said coldly. "We heard he'd been *messing around* with you and Keri."

"Among others, as we found out. Our boy Jed is a real player." Lucy smirked.

Shannen stared at her, nonplussed. "You don't mind that you've been, uh, played?"

"Why should guys have all the fun? We girls can, too, you know. Being here is like a vacation fling, we may as well enjoy ourselves." Lucy followed a hiccup with a giggle. "It's all in the game, you know?"

No, it was worse than "the game" of *Victorious,* Shannen mused bleakly. Lucy was describing a game of men and women sleeping together, using each other and openly not caring about the lack of…well, caring.

As if that weren't bad enough, it sounded like the perfidious Jed was not only boasting about his conquests, he was making them up and including Lauren in his tally. The gossip about her twin and Jed just *had* to be unfounded. Surely the only game Lauren was playing was *Victorious*.

Listening to Lucy's breezy assessment of the casual bed hopping sent Shannen's anxiety level soaring higher. She'd hopped into bed with Ty last night—twice!—without a single word of commitment, before or afterward, from either of them. As if it were nothing more than a vacation fling.

Maybe that's all it was for Ty? He wanted her, sure. But Jed wanted Lucy and Keri, and they weren't even pretending it went any deeper than that. Shannen thought of what she felt for Ty both before and after making love with him, of the words she'd wanted to say but hadn't. She had muzzled herself, and deep in her heart had believed that Ty was doing and feeling the same.

What if he wasn't? She flinched at that heartbreaking possibility.

"I came to ask you to have dinner and go to the Parrot Room with the gang tonight." Lucy's voice broke into Shannen's troubled reverie.

"Thanks, but I think I'll—" Shannen paused, trying to come up with an excuse that at least sounded viable. "I'm still tired, and I'll just eat in my room and go to bed early," she added lamely.

"Oh, come with us, you'll have fun," urged Lucy. "We all feel sorry for you, sitting here by yourself looking so glum. We know how much you miss your twin."

Shannen stiffened. "You feel sorry for me?"

"It's so sad! You and your sister are like together all the time for your whole life, and now you're here and she's over there and you—"

"We're not Siamese twins, we can exist apart from each other," Shannen interjected, stung.

The idea of the group feeling sorry for her because she and Lauren had been apart for less than twenty-four hours offended her greatly.

Part of her wanted to blurt out that she was sitting here

by herself looking so glum because she didn't know if the man she loved was in love with her or simply in lust.

Being Shannen, she would never make such a heartfelt confession.

"I'll hang out with the gang tonight," she said instead. "Thanks for including me."

Ty glanced at his watch for perhaps the tenth time in the past half hour. It must not be working; perhaps the sand and/or salt air had taken its toll.

But a check with Heidi confirmed his watch was up-to-the-second correct, and Ty faced facts. Time had not slowed to a halt, but his tolerance for his job had.

He did not want to be here; he wanted to be with Shannen. In her room in the hotel making love or sitting on the balcony with her chatting while they ate. Just being with her, doing anything at all, was preferable to being apart from her, especially after last night.

Instead he was here, trapped in a time warp of tedium, filming the Final Four contestants, Lauren, Cortnee, Konrad and Rico. Each one was posed, sitting or standing in a different setting while reciting a soliloquy about his or her feelings on making it this far in the game.

"Clark Garrett and the network can kiss their dreams of a *Victorious* franchise goodbye after broadcasting the banal blatherings of the Final Four," Ty muttered as Rico droned on. "This isn't merely dull, it's coma inducing."

"Maybe editing will help?" Heidi offered hopefully. "Why doesn't Clark or Bobby have them do something besides sit around and talk?"

"Cortnee's not even wearing her bikini," lamented Reggie. "And it's a shame the evil twin isn't the one who's still here. Wouldn't she have snarled at having to do these inane monologues! That would've been fun to see. Instead, we have the bland twin, who just simpers."

Ty thought how much Shannen would hate to hear as-

persions cast against Lauren, who in reality wasn't bland
at all. Just as Shannen was no evil twin. So much for reality
shows being real.

But he agreed with Reggie on one point. Shannen's fire
would've definitely livened up the glacial pace of the so-
liloquies. Shannen could never be boring.

He'd told her so last night, on the balcony.

You're incapable of boring me, Shannen. He was glad
he'd at least said that, because there was much more he
had kept from her. Things she deserved to hear, like his
feelings for her. Things she ought to know, like his true
financial status.

Last night she'd told him candidly that she preferred him
without wealth. Without his "money issues," as she'd
phrased it. Well, thanks to wise investing, he had more
money now than when they had first met.

He could undoubtedly write a check covering what her
family needed from his personal bank account. The diner
repairs, the grandmother's house and the older sister's
fledgling lawn business might seem insurmountably high to
the Cullens, but not to him. He wouldn't even have to tap
into his money-market funds or touch his major liquid as-
sets for such a minor sum.

Suppose he were to offer to do it? He could make it an
outright gift or a loan with no interest and no deadline to
pay it back. Such a sum wouldn't even make a dent in his
portfolio.

Ty tried to imagine Shannen's reaction if he were to
make such an offer. And found that he couldn't.

Would she be delirious with joy, and then proceed to
show him just how happy she was with him and his money?
Or would she be angry at him for lying to her—and then
make him work mightily to convince her to accept his
generosity?

Shannen had said having money made him paranoid
about being valued for himself. She certainly had a point

there, Ty conceded. And when the notorious Howe scandals had hit, one after the other, he'd bailed on the name.

Had that been a mistake, a step into the world of denial instead of the smart self-defensive move he'd considered it to be? Until this minute he'd never even thought to question it.

Yet it helped immensely that Shannen already knew him as a Howe and didn't judge him as one. He'd kept his distance from everyone in his new life, not trusting anyone to accept him for who and what he really was.

Now he was playing his Trust No One game with Shannen herself by not being truthful about his "money issues."

Bobby arrived to announce another immunity contest. "You might be familiar with this one." He beamed at the camera.

Four wooden beams were being placed upright in the water—one for each of the contestants to stand on. It was an endurance test, and the last one left standing won immunity from being voted off the island.

"Familiar with it?" Ty muttered. "This stunt was a staple of the earliest game shows, and it was tired even back then. Not to mention about as interesting as watching paint dry."

"No, watching paint dry is way more interesting," Heidi countered snidely.

"These kids are young and strong. It'll be hours before one of them feels the need to move a limb." Reggie groaned. "They'll time-lapse the footage for the show, but we're stuck filming in real time."

"What am I doing here?" Ty asked himself. "I'm thirty-four years old. Why am I living in a bug-ridden camp with kids years younger than me, filming wannabe celebs who will do anything for a buck?"

"I hear you." Reggie was sympathetic. "Hang in there, friend. Better gigs are on the horizon—they have to be."

Ty was disconcerted to realize he'd spoken his thoughts

aloud. Truly a sign of how agitated he really was. He angled his camera to zoom in on a close-up of Konrad, who looked completely relaxed standing on the pole in the ocean.

He was a lawyer, Ty admonished himself, though silently this time. He should be practicing law, not holding a camera on a contestant in a game show. It was the first time he'd questioned his choice of a new career since leaving behind the world of Howe.

All lawyers didn't have to be corrupt and unethical like his father and uncle, just as all accountants weren't scheming thieves like his brother. He could choose to put his law degree and his talents toward a good cause.

With his personal fortune, he wouldn't have to take on cases for the money they would bring, which meant eliminating the criminal element and concentrating on those truly in need of legal assistance.

He could open his own practice or work for a nonprofit legal aid organization. He could buy a house and settle down instead of traipsing from efficiency apartments and rented rooms while chasing camerawork on random shows.

It seemed like an appealing alternative to what he was doing now. Why hadn't he thought of this before?

Ty fixed his camera on Lauren and wished she were Shannen, puzzling over why people had such a difficult time telling the sisters apart. Shannen was unique, remarkable, unmistakably herself.

What was she doing right now? he wondered. Was she looking forward to seeing him tonight? He allowed himself to anticipate their reunion, his mind blissfully detached from the Final Four as his camera rolled on.

Six hours of standing out in the sun on the post finally reduced Cortnee to tears. All four contestants had consistently refused Bobby's serpent-in-the-garden-like temptations to quit the contest and be rewarded with food and drink.

Ty didn't admire their stamina so much as question their sanity. He began to feel guilty filming them, as if he were aiding and abetting torture. They weren't even allowed a sip of water unless they abandoned their stance, thus forfeiting a chance to win the contest.

For six endless hours, none of them would yield. If one of the contestants were to drop dead, he could help the bereaved kin file a wrongful death suit, Ty decided, not entirely facetiously. And he wouldn't charge a penny for it.

Lauren and Cortnee continued to wilt before the camera lens, and Rico looked increasingly uncomfortable. Only Konrad was stoic, his demeanor unchanged from when he first climbed atop the post.

"I can't do this anymore!" Cortnee cried at last. "If I get down, can I have some water and that avocado salad you offered me a while ago, Bobby?"

"You certainly can!" Bobby assured her unctuously. "Plus, I'll throw in any kind of sandwich and dessert that you want, too. As much as you want of everything. Have I made you an offer you can't refuse?"

Sobbing, Cortnee jumped off and swam the short distance to the shore.

The roar of a high-powered speedboat engine was a jarring invasion into the quiet of the waning afternoon. Ty stopped his camera even before the shouted order, "Cut!"

All filming ceased.

"Say, that's one of the hotel's boats!" exclaimed Bobby, rising from his shaded deck chair. "It must be Clark bringing the network suits over for a look-see. I guess they want to meet us." He smoothed an imaginary wrinkle from his impeccably pressed shirt and ordered Heidi to bring him a mirror and comb.

Everybody watched as Clark Garrett and two older men

dressed untropically in business-casual wear disembarked from the boat, which had retractable wheels to drive it right onto the shore. The driver of the boat, a hotel employee, tied the boat to a stake, something of a primitive makeshift dock.

"As if this day weren't long enough," growled Ty. "Now it's going to be truly interminable."

There were groans of assent from the production assistants.

A far worse thought struck Ty. If the network executives were here on the island to watch the filming, there would be no need to take the day's footage to the hotel for them to view tonight. No reason to leave the crew camp for the resort. And no opportunity to see Shannen.

If he couldn't see Shannen tonight...

Ty resisted the urge to quit on the spot. He could buy that stupid boat and take it to the hotel right now. Neither his father nor his brother would hesitate to make such a flamboyant scene. They would even suggest a cameraman record the drama. It was that horrific flash of insight that kept Ty from acting it out.

And then...

"Lauren!"

Shannen? Ty was glad he'd put down his camera, because he probably would've dropped it at the sound of Shannen's voice. He wasn't delusional—it was really her!

She'd come out of the boat's cabin and stood on the small deck to wave at her sister, a few yards out in the water.

"Shannen! I can't believe it! You're here!" Lauren cried from her post.

Ty couldn't have said it better himself.

"These guys were nice enough to let me hitch a ride over with them." Shannen grinned as she hopped off the boat onto the sand.

She was wearing a blue paisley sundress, and it looked

as clean and crisp as one of Bobby Dixon's ensembles. Her hair swung loose around her shoulders and was ruffled by the breeze.

At the sight of her, Ty's blood grew hot. Every muscle in his body tightened as a surge of erotically charged memories flooded him. And then she removed her sunglasses, revealing eyes alert and shining with intelligence and—when she spotted him—something more.

Warmth. Humor. Tenderness. Was it possible to see such things in someone's gaze or was he projecting what he wanted, what he *needed*, to be there?

Ty walked toward her. Everybody was milling around; the production assistants bringing food and water to Cortnee, the rest of the crew taking a break with snacks or cigarettes while Bobby, Clark Garrett and the network execs toured the area.

Ty didn't care if everybody on the island was watching as he came to stand by Shannen's side. "You must know how glad I am to see you."

"Must I?" She shot him a quick smile before turning to look out at Lauren, Rico and Konrad standing on the posts. "How long have they been out there?"

"Over six hours. Cortnee just gave it up. Poor kid."

They both glanced at Cortnee, who was draining a bottle of cold water. Adam was fanning her with a large palm frond.

"Poor kid is right," agreed Shannen. "And if she gets voted off today, she won't even have the fun of living it up at the resort till the end of the game."

Ty wanted to take her hand and pull her into his arms. The hell with keeping secrets! There was no reason to pretend there was nothing between them, no reason for the pretense of a casual conversation between cameraman and ineligible contestant.

But he resisted the urge and didn't make his move. Shannen was standing beside him, not close enough for their shoulders to touch or their hands to brush. She was looking around at the Final Four, not up at him, sending clear non-verbal messages to keep up the pretense.

"Why won't Cortnee have fun at the resort?" Ty quizzed instead.

Maybe he couldn't touch her, but at least she was here to talk to. Her presence brought an end to the teeth-gnashing frustration he'd been suffering all day. With Shannen at his side, not even watching paint dry would be intolerable.

"What's not fun about an all-expense-paid stay in tropical luxury?" he prompted.

"Well, it's still tropical but not so luxurious now," said Shannen. "Lucy and the others say the network bosses turned the resort into a gulag."

"How is that possible? Last night—"

"—was the end of the good times. Apparently, the network bosses wigged out at the size of the bill the group has been running up at the resort."

"So that's why they look so grim." Ty glanced at the unsmiling network execs tramping around the camp. "Hmm, maybe *grim* is too upbeat a word to describe them."

"True. Clark Garrett called everybody together after lunch and screamed at us for almost an hour," said Shannen. "He claimed he'd been screamed at even longer by the network brass. They were *not* happy that the contestants and staffers at the hotel have all been ordering four and five of the most expensive appetizers and entrées apiece in the restaurants at every meal, plus the room service bills were astronomical."

"Having been to the Parrot Room to collect Kevin and Adam last night, and knowing that the group hung out there every night, I'm guessing the bar bill alone would've been enough to send the honchos into orbit," Ty mused.

"And then they found out about all the charges at the

spa and the gift shop," added Shannen. "I thought Uncle Clark was going to kill Miles right in front of us."

"Well, Miles was the one encouraging everybody to get everything. Too bad they got greedy."

"I was in the gift shop today. They charge five dollars for a pack of gum and two hundred dollars for a T-shirt with the resort logo," Shannen marveled.

"Everybody in the *Victorious* group had on one of those last night at the Parrot Room. We're talking a few thousand in T-shirts right there." Ty laughed. "No wonder Uncle Clark—"

"Had homicide in his heart," Shannen put in slyly. "And before you can ask, no, I didn't buy anything in the gift shop, and I was there before the ban was imposed. The five dollars for gum struck me as high-end robbery. Gramma sells gum for fifty cents a pack at the diner."

"The prices at the resort are inflated, all right." Ty thought of the overpriced box of condoms he'd purchased there. Not that they weren't worth it, of course.

A sudden gust of wind sent Shannen's skirt billowing, and she quickly pushed it down—but not before he'd caught a glimpse of her shapely tanned thigh. Last night he'd seen so much more....

He stared at Shannen, his gaze intimate, possessive. Thinking back on last night, would it really have been the end of the world if he had made her pregnant? He must've thought so when he plunked down twenty bucks for the box of condoms.

But today he reconsidered. Making her pregnant would be the end of the world as he knew it, but suddenly that didn't strike him as a bad thing. Perhaps he should've bought four packs of the overpriced gum instead, because the concept of Shannen carrying his child enticed him.

"Anyway, Clark issued the official network decree," Shannen continued, oblivious of Ty's startling yet irresistible daydream. "Starting this afternoon, the network will pay only for the rooms, plus twenty-five dollars a day per person for food. No room service, no drinks at the bar, no spa or gift-shop charges. Nothing extra.''

"Twenty-five dollars a day for food at those hotel prices isn't very much,'' Ty observed.

"True, considering a cheeseburger is one of the cheapest things on the menu and costs twelve dollars. A cola is six dollars. That's what I had for lunch before the boom was lowered. Guess I should've gone for the lobster and imported white asparagus instead, huh?''

"I understand why they've made restrictions, but their food allowance is pretty draconian, considering there's no alternative place to eat on that island.'' Ty frowned. "After your nonnutritional sojourn here, you should be eating three decent meals a day, and you can't do that over there on twenty-five dollars a day.''

"I'll manage.'' Shannen dismissed his concern and waved to Lauren, who couldn't seem to summon the energy to wave back.

Shannen turned worriedly to Ty. "How much longer do you think they'll last out there?''

"That's anybody's guess, but I think Konrad will win. Lauren and Rico are definitely showing signs of weakening, but Konrad looks the same as when this madness began.''

"Hey, everybody! Break's over, start filming again,'' called the assistant director.

Ty and the others retrieved their cameras. Reggie focused on Cortnee, who was feasting on an avocado salad and barbecued chicken; Ty turned his camera on the three stalwart contestants who remained in the competition.

Shannen continued to stand beside him, and nobody commented on it. Nobody even glanced their way.

"I like the freedom of being a reject,'' she decided. "It's like being invisible. And it sure beats standing on a beam out there. Poor Lauren! Besides being tired and thirsty, I can't imagine how bored she must be.''

"I can. I was as bored as they are. Until you showed up, that is."

He shifted, moving imperceptibly until his hip grazed hers. The contact would look accidental if anybody were watching. He waited for Shannen's reaction. Would she move away or stay where she was, their bodies discreetly touching?

Ty was elated when she remained there, although she didn't acknowledge their proximity. She put her sunglasses back on and continued to look straight ahead at the contest in the sea.

Ty kept one eye on his subjects and one on Shannen. It felt so right to have her here with him. And they were on the same side of the camera at last! She was adorable, she was feisty, she was passionate and funny and down-to-earth. He yearned to tell her so—if only they were alone.

But they weren't, and he knew this was neither the time nor the place for a truly private conversation. Someone could join them at any minute and undoubtedly would. So he would stick to impersonal topics.

"I'm curious how you managed to nab a ride over here with Clark and the network bosses, Shannen," he said conversationally. "Considering their outrage over the bills, I can't seeing them eager to grant any favors to the *Victorious* cast."

"They aren't mad at me," Shannen said succinctly. "Since I was the newest to arrive on the island, I didn't have a chance to run up a big bill. I put all the food from the room fridge back in it, so I didn't get charged for that, and my only room service meal was the turkey sandwich. I slept through breakfast and had the cheeseburger for lunch. And I had no gift shop purchases."

She flashed a mischievous smile. "Ed—he's the one in the pale-peach shirt talking to Bobby—was ready to canonize me when he saw my expenses. Or lack of them."

"And what made you decide to join them on a visit over

to the old camp?'' Ty parried lightly. ''Didn't like the idea of lounging around a cushy resort, huh?''

''The other contestants thought I was suffering from separation anxiety because Lauren and I weren't together.'' Shannen matched the breeziness of his tone. ''I wanted to come here, so I decided to pretend to be the pathetic misfit they already thought I was.''

''The have-the-name-might-as-well-play-the-game strategy. A classic. Been in use since biblical times, I believe.''

''Maybe even earlier.'' Shannen laughed a little. ''I told Clark I had to see my sister because I was having twin vibes that something was wrong. He assured me Lauren was fine, but he invited me to come along and see for myself.''

''Is there any truth to the twin separation anxiety, Shannen?'' Ty asked quietly. ''You're not a pathetic misfit for worrying about your sister, you know.''

''I thought about Lauren, of course, especially with that snake Jed spreading those rumors.'' She scowled her disapproval. ''But Lauren and I have been apart before. Not often, but it's happened. We don't collapse when we're out of each other's sight.''

''Let me see if I have the facts straight, Shannen. You wanted to come here, but you weren't pining away for a glimpse of your twin, even though you let Clark think so. Interesting.''

''Isn't it?'' Shannen gave his foot a slight nudge with her own.

''Is this the part where I'm supposed to guess why you're really here?'' Ty asked huskily.

She nodded, flushing from head to toe, knowing the sudden rush of heat was unrelated to the tropical sun. Ty's dark eyes seemed to look inside of her. She felt exposed and vulnerable and was grateful that her sunglasses prevented him from reading her emotions in her eyes.

Had she made a major tactical error in showing up here

on the island today? Ty had looked very pleased to see her, but maybe any man would get an ego boost at the sight of his previous night's conquest.

She'd acted on impulse today, but when it came to her behavior with Ty, that was par for the course. He seemed to activate impulsivity in her...along with many other feelings.

"Here's my first guess, Shannen. Maybe you'd like to hear me admit that your appearance here is most timely?" Ty paraphrased himself from last night, his voice wry.

Shannen felt as if fireworks were going off in her head. Besieged with uncertainty, she knew if he'd made some cocky sexual comeback about his prowess and her craving for him, she would have gone as nuclear as the network executives facing the expense tally.

And then she would've had to grapple with being wounded by his insensitivity and arrogance. Been there, done that, nine years ago, even though he'd thought he was being noble. And nine years ago there had been no sexual intimacy between them to make the pain ever sharper. This time around...

Thank heavens they were more in sync this time around! His gently humorous reply validated her instincts for coming here.

"Your first guess is right," she said softly.

A broad grin creased his face. "I admit it, your appearance here is most timely, Shannen."

"Wow! That's the truth!" Heidi joined them just in time to catch the end of his remark. "You really must have that twin ESP going on strong! You *knew* your sister needed you!"

Heidi pointed to Lauren, who was swaying perilously, gripping the pole with both arms. Moments later she slipped off the post into the water.

Before anyone on the beach could react, Rico jumped in after her and pulled her to her feet.

"Just keep filming!" shouted Clark. "Nobody go in the water! The girl's okay, and we don't want to ruin the drama by cluttering up the scene with the crew."

Shannen ignored him and ran into the water, sandals and all. Within a split second, Heidi caught up to her and grabbed her arm, following another order from Clark.

Shannen began to struggle. "Get away from me!"

"You're not even supposed to be here," exclaimed Heidi, trying harder to hold her back. "Tell her, Ty," she pleaded to Ty, who'd followed them both.

"Tell her not to go to her sister who practically fainted in the water?" snarled Ty. "Forget it." He handed the camera to Kevin, who had raced in, too. "I'm not filming this."

Shannen successfully broke free from Heidi and ran toward Lauren and Rico. The pair were approaching the shore, hanging on to each other. Both looked fatigued and sunburned, and it was hard to tell who was supporting whom.

Shannen threw her arms around them both. "Oh, Lauren, you poor thing! And, Rico, you're a hero for jumping in after her like that, without even thinking twice."

"We got that part on film," Reggie called.

"Thank God! The rest we'll have to edit out," announced Clark. "Pan to Cortnee and to Konrad."

Cortnee held her hands to her cheeks and looked tearful.

Konrad was smiling. "I'm the last one standing, so I win immunity."

Shannen barely heard him as she prepared to tell Clark Garrett exactly what she thought of him.

Nine

The network executives wanted to watch the tribal council in person, so Shannen would stay on the island until they all returned to the resort by boat later in the evening. The contestant who was voted off would go with them.

"Keep that crazy twin out of camera range," Clark said to Ty. "Put her on a leash if you have to, just don't let her get filmed by mistake. Editing can only fix so much."

Clark wiped sweat from his brow with his already-damp handkerchief. He was looking haggard after an encounter with the enraged Shannen. Brimming with white-hot rage, she had reviled him, quite effectively, in front of everybody.

Ty, who had witnessed many a verbal annihilation directed at the Howes, recognized her as a true master of the art.

Silence had descended, and not even Bobby Dixon tried to deliver one of his annoying platitudes. Nobody cared to risk incurring the wrath of Shannen.

When she'd proclaimed, "Somebody better get my sister and Rico something to eat and drink right now!" even the network executives hurried to fetch food and water.

"Ty, I want you to know I appreciate you going into the water to try to stop that demented bitch from ruining the terrific scene of the two losers staggering in together," continued Clark. "*Twins!* Who knew they'd go psycho? We won't be casting twins in *Victorious Two,* I can promise you that."

Ty shook his head. He was disgusted with Clark's callousness toward Lauren's fall into the water, and to make matters worse, the obtuse executive producer had misinterpreted his lunge into the water after Shannen.

Ty had gone in to help her with Lauren, to show his support for her, not to restrain her, as that blockhead Garrett believed.

But Shannen hadn't needed Ty's intervention and refused it when he offered.

"We're fine. Go back and get your camera," she told him, slipping her arm around Lauren. "You'll get in trouble. Clark is throwing a tantrum as it is and—"

"Screw Clark Garrett!" cursed Ty.

Shannen flashed a sardonic smile. "I'd rather not."

Ty arched his brows. "You'd better not!"

Rico and Lauren laughed weakly.

And then the production assistants hauled away the two contestants, leaving Shannen and Ty to wade ashore together.

"Ty, seriously, you have to do your job," said Shannen. "You have to start filming or else—"

"I could be fired? I'm so worried." Ty was sarcastic.

"We all have these take-this-job-and-shove-it moments, Tynan," Shannen explained patiently. "And everybody has had at least one boss who's a jerk, but—"

"Shannen, I'll get my camera and film the contestants, but please dispense with the pep talk," growled Ty.

It was bad enough he was trapped in his own stupid deception. Hearing her try to console him about it made him queasy with guilt. He had too many deceptions going on in his life—his name, his career and his past relationship with Shannen.

Only she knew most of the truth, but he'd kept a vital fact from her too: his wealth.

How to tell her? *When* to tell her? Because he knew now that he wanted her to know the full truth.

Shannen, unaware of his dilemma, thought he was still mired in a take-this-job-and-shove-it moment.

She gave him a bolstering thumbs-up and headed toward Lauren and Rico, who were guzzling bottles of water.

Now it was time for the voting, and as the Final Four sat in the tribal council area, Bobby delivered a ponderous homily about four being narrowed to three.

Konrad clutched the immunity totem as if it were a priceless antiquity. Lauren, Rico and Cortnee looked tense and eyed each other warily.

Shannen stood next to Ty as he filmed. "It's kind of sad," she whispered to him. "I remember when those four were a solid alliance, maybe even friends. Well, sort of. But now they don't trust each other."

"It was inevitable, Shannen. They're each playing for themselves now."

"I know, I know." She sighed. "It's all in the game."

She saw Clark Garrett and the production assistants stealing nervous glances at her. And she noticed for the first time that the entire crew had taken positions well away from her and Ty.

"I see you've been chosen to be the human sacrifice and rein me in, should I suddenly go berserk," Shannen mocked, her eyes locking with Clark Garrett's.

It gave her a naughty thrill to see him brace himself, as

if expecting her to suddenly fly at him like a rabid vampire bat.

"Stop terrorizing Clark, Shannen," Ty admonished dryly. "You've already carved him up with that sharp little tongue of yours once today, and he's dreading another attack."

"My verbal skills have advanced beyond trite kid stuff like 'condescending, self-righteous jerk,' haven't they?" Shannen was pleased.

"Well beyond, honey. Remind me not to cross you."

"I will," she replied playfully. "Every chance I get."

"It's time to vote," Bobby's voice boomed, drowning out even their muffled whispers.

"Uh-oh!" Shannen's lighthearted mood evaporated. She met Lauren's eyes and held up her hand, her two fingers crossed for good luck.

Lauren bit her lip and looked away.

As always, the votes against each contestant were announced by Bobby with melodramatic flair.

"Cortnee." He held up a card and read the name.

From her position behind the camera, Shannen saw the voting cards for the first time. She recognized Lauren's handwriting immediately.

"Lauren," read Bobby, and Shannen thought the penmanship on that card looked girlishly embellished. The way Cortnee might write?

"I think the two girls just canceled out each other's votes," she whispered to Ty, who made no comment. "They should've stuck together."

"Rico," Bobby's voice boomed, and he held up a card with printing so atrocious, Shannen guessed it to be Konrad's. He'd often boasted of his school failures, and perhaps printing was one of them.

"Three votes for three different people." Bobby stated the obvious.

Shannen resisted the urge to rush him and snatch the remaining card from his hand.

"This is the last vote, and the name I read will be the person who will extinguish their flashlight and leave the island," Bobby intoned solemnly.

Dragging out the moment with agonizing slowness, he studied the card. Finally, *finally* he read it: "Lauren."

Shannen and Lauren each drew in a short, sharp breath, then simultaneously schooled their expressions into smiles of acceptance.

Ty watched, his eyes darting from sister to sister, fascinated by their identical responses.

One camera lingered an extra few moments on Lauren, but her smile didn't falter. Ty filmed Cortnee hugging Rico and then Konrad in turn.

"I'm sorry, sweetie," Ty whispered to Shannen.

She shrugged. "We were lucky to make it this far. And Lauren will win five thousand dollars for being the fourth of the Final Four. That's great!"

She gave him such a sunny smile, he felt perversely glum. Would five thousand dollars after taxes be enough to even fix their grandmother's roof, let alone cover the diner's expenses?

"Anyway, Jordan can keep on buying those powerball tickets," Shannen said, even more brightly.

"Shannen, it's okay to express disappointment," Ty murmured. "You don't have to put on a front with me."

The camera recorded Lauren extinguishing her flashlight and then turned to focus on the others. Immediately afterward, Lauren rushed over to Shannen and began to cry.

"Oh, Shan, I'm so sorry! I should've given you the immunity thing instead of keeping it for myself. You never would've fallen off the post. And nobody would've voted against you, either. I'm such a flop!"

"Lauren, no! You are not!" Shannen hugged her sister and rocked her in her arms. "You played a good game.

We both did. It was even fun, in a hellish kind of way, wasn't it?''

"It was horrible!" Lauren wept. "I wish we'd never come here, I wish I hadn't dragged you to the audition. Oh, Shannen, I just want to go home!"

Heidi approached, giving Ty an apprehensive look. "It's time to get Lauren's things and for both of them to leave the island." Heidi addressed Ty instead of the twins.

"I'll take them," offered Ty and stepped between the sisters, holding a twin with each arm. "Let's go."

Everyone's eyes were upon them.

"The crew is looking at you like you singlehandedly tamed the shrew," Shannen said as they walked along the path to the camp. "Was I *that* scary when I yelled at Clark Garrett? The heartless boor could run the ice concession in hell," she added fiercely.

"You made an impressive show of fury unbound," Ty allowed, his eyes gleaming. "But you didn't scare me. It takes a lot to scare me, Shannen."

"I'll keep that in mind, Tynan."

"Are you two ever going to tell me how you know each other?" Lauren had stopped crying and was watching them.

Shannen and Ty exchanged glances.

"We'll get back to you on that one," said Ty, speaking for them both.

The network executives were impatient to leave the island for the resort and insisted that Clark Garrett hurry the twins along. He did, but with obvious trepidation.

"All of a sudden I feel like we're moving at warp speed," complained Ty as he walked with Shannen to the boat.

Lauren, clutching her few possessions, was a few feet ahead of them with Clark. The network bosses and the driver were already in the boat.

"While we were filming the immunity contest, time crawled by," Ty continued to gripe. "Why do some hours have sixty thousand minutes in them and other hours are only sixty seconds long?''

"If you don't mind me quoting Gramma again, 'Time flies when you're having fun,''' said Shannen. "Although I'm not sure if it applies here. Watching Lauren collapse into the water and then get voted off the island wasn't fun.''

"No, but being with you is,'' Ty countered huskily. "Even under these less-than-ideal circumstances.''

"I'm glad I came today,'' she said.

Her words, her tone, were almost perfunctory. Ty sensed her withdrawal increasing in direct proportion to their nearness to the boat.

The frustration within him soared to this morning's high, before Shannen's appearance on the island. Maybe even higher, because he knew there would be no surprise visit by her tomorrow. She couldn't play the twin separation card because Lauren would be with her.

When was he going to see her again? Not knowing was intolerable!

"Come onboard, young lady!'' Ed, the network executive in the pale-peach shirt, shouted from the boat.

Clark Garrett and Lauren had just boarded, and the driver revved up the engine.

"I'll get the crew boat and come to your room tonight,'' Ty said quickly.

"Ty, you can't.'' Shannen gazed up at him, her blue eyes wide. "You won't be allowed to go—there's no film to take to the network bosses. They've been here all day.''

"I won't be marooned on this stupid island simply because I don't have an official okay to leave.''

"But, Ty, if you don't have permission to take the boat, you—''

"Permission?'' Ty repeated scornfully. "I'm taking the boat, with or without *permission*.''

"That's Tynan Howe talking, not Ty Hale,'' reproved

Shannen. "You might've been able to do as you pleased when you were rich, but now you have to..."

"...take orders from idiots like Clark Garrett and those network stooges?" Ty was incensed. "I could buy and sell all three, many times over!"

"Not any longer." Shannen laid her hand on his arm. "That was then, Ty. This is now," she reminded him gently. "Now you work for them and—"

"Shannen, they're ready to go," called Lauren.

Ty exhaled sharply. "Shannen—"

"Ty, even if you did manage to come to the resort tonight, I wouldn't let you in my room," Shannen's voice was low and urgent. "Because—"

"Oh, of course, there's Lauren," Ty said. "We'll get her a room of her own. Don't worry, I'll pay for it myself."

"It's not because Lauren will be sharing my room, Ty. I've done a lot of thinking since last night and I...I decided that I can't go to bed with you again." She expelled her declaration in a breathless rush.

"What?" Ty felt as though he'd been clubbed over the head.

Maybe he had been. Maybe Konrad had sneaked up and whacked him with the immunity totem.

He must've sustained a substantial blow, because he seemingly had lost the powers of comprehension. Shannen couldn't have said what he'd just heard.

"Last night we went too far too fast, Ty." She sounded tense and edgy. "We have to slow down, to back up and...and get to know each other."

"Shannen, one thing we can't be accused of is rushing things. We've known each other for nine years!"

"When you put it like that—"

"It sounds ridiculous? That's because it is, Shannen!"

"No, it sounds like a twisted argument. We *knew* each other nine years ago, Ty. That's a big difference from *knowing* each other for that long. We parted on bad terms and we certainly didn't keep in touch. When we remet here on the island, it was like two strangers meeting for the first time."

"Keep in touch?" echoed Ty. "Is this retaliation for not calling you on your twenty-first birthday? I explained why I thought you wouldn't want to hear from me at that time. Or any time after. As for being strangers to each other—"

The boat horn blasted, sounding as loud as the start at the Indy 500, drowning him out.

"The very fact you assumed I wouldn't want to hear from you simply proves my point about not knowing each other very well," Shannen said urgently. "Not then or now. And I have to go before they break the sound barrier again with that awful horn."

Ty gripped her shoulders. "Shannen, we can't leave things this way." He wondered if he sounded as desperate as he felt. "I won't let you end it and just walk away."

"Ty—"

"Which is what I did nine years ago," he admitted grimly. "And even knowing that I took the high moral ground back then is no consolation now, Shannen. If you wanted revenge, baby, you've got it."

"Will you stop jumping to stupid conclusions and just shut up and listen to me for a minute?" Shannen's temper flared. "I'm not out for revenge, and if you actually believe that, you've once again proved that you don't know me." Her voice softened. "But I want you to, Ty. Let me put it into TV terms you'll understand. I'm putting sex on hiatus, not canceling our relationship. If you can't accept that…"

The ear-splitting boat horn blared again. Shannen pulled away from him and ran to the boat.

"It's about time," grumbled the other network executive, the one who wasn't Ed. "What was going on, anyway?"

"I was thanking Mr. Hale for being kind to me today," Shannen replied demurely. "I'm most appreciative, especially after Clark Garrett's attitude toward my sister's fall. His lack of concern bordered on negligence!"

"I wasn't—" Clark started, but Shannen cut him right off.

"Just thinking about it made me furious all over again, and Mr. Hale was trying to persuade me not to commandeer this boat on the way back and kick Clark Garrett overboard."

"Oh," both network execs chorused. They glanced uneasily at the driver, who paid no attention to the conversation going on.

"Don't worry, Mr. Hale convinced me not to do it." Shannen was all smiles and reassurance. "You really ought to think about giving him a raise, if you value Clark Garrett. Because Ty Hale saved him from being shark food."

"What were you and Ty really talking about back on the beach, Shannen?" Lauren asked as the twins entered the hotel lobby. Clark and the bosses were far ahead of them. "And don't give me that lunatic story that he convinced you not to hijack the boat and throw Clark Garrett to the sharks."

"Actually, he told me to go ahead and do it. That I'd be making the world a better place. And then we could toss Slick Bobby overboard tomorrow night," Shannen said flippantly.

"Shannen!"

"Lauren!"

The twins held one of their familiar face-offs, then grinned at each other.

"I'm so glad you're here, Lauren." Shannen gave her sister a small squeeze. "You'll like our room. It's pure heaven to take a long, hot shower, and the bed is king-size and like sleeping on a cloud. Tomorrow we'll go to the pool and—"

"Shannen, look, there's Jed!" Lauren exclaimed. "He's

over there with the others by the entrance to that hallway. Let's go say hello.''

Shannen saw the nervous excitement light Lauren's face, and gulped back an exclamation of dismay. ''Why not wait till tomorrow, Lauren? After you've had a shower and a good night's sleep.''

And I've had a chance to try and talk some sense into you, she added silently.

Jed was standing among the other ousted *Victorious* contestants and hadn't seen them yet, but Lauren was quick to change that. She bolted across the lobby.

Shannen felt she had no choice but to go after her. ''Lauren, just play it cool,'' she whispered as they approached the group.

Lauren made no reply.

Shannen watched her sister closely and proceeded to duplicate her every move and every nuance of expression. It was a skill they'd perfected back when they were kids, and confusing people was a fun game.

Right now it was a necessity, Shannen decided grimly. If Jed couldn't tell who was who, she doubted he would risk making a play for Lauren. The rat would be too afraid he might be hitting on the Scary Twin, the one who'd had ''homicide in her heart'' last night.

''Hi, Jed,'' Lauren said, slightly breathless.

''Hi Jed,'' Shannen imitated her twin right down to the appealing head tilt. She wanted to laugh out loud at the look of sheer panic that crossed Jed's face as his eyes darted from one sister to the other.

And then he smiled directly, confidently at Lauren.

''Well, hello there, Lauren. And welcome! Can I help you with this?'' Jed offered to take Lauren's things, which she'd almost dropped while hurrying across the lobby.

''Thanks, Jed.'' Lauren gave him a dreamy smile.

For a moment Shannen was too stunned to react at all. How had Jed known which one of them was Lauren? He certainly couldn't tell last night when he'd drunkenly barged into her room.

She looked at her sister, who was handing her bundle of belongings to Jed. And realized how he'd suddenly acquired the ability to differentiate between them.

Lauren was wearing the shorts and triangle top she'd worn during much of the *Victorious* filming, Shannen was in a sundress. Nobody wore dresses at camp on the island.

And while Shannen had enjoyed the luxury of a leisurely shower and shampoo in her private bathroom this morning, Lauren had to make do with the meager spring on the island.

A moment later Miles joined the group, no longer the effervescent lad who had greeted Shannen yesterday. He was subdued and sullen, the result of a scathing lecture from his uncle Clark and the network bosses, Shannen assumed.

"I'll take you to your room," Miles said flatly, making none of yesterday's grandiose offers. "You're sharing it with your sister. You can order something from the room service menu as long as it costs under twenty-five dollars, tip included."

"I know where the room is. I can take her there," Shannen volunteered.

"I have a better idea," said Jed. He turned to Shannen and dumped Lauren's things in her arms. "You take these to the room, and I'll go with Lauren to the coffee shop where she can order something—under twenty-five dollars, Miles." He winked at the production assistant. "Then I'll show you around the hotel, Lauren."

"That sounds wonderful!" Lauren beamed up at him.

"No, it doesn't!" Shannen snapped. "Lauren, you—"

"It's okay, I'll come up later, Shan. Don't worry, I'll find my way." Lauren took another small step closer to Jed. "Oh, and thanks for taking my stuff to the room, Shannen."

Jed slipped his arm around Lauren's waist and whisked her off. "She'll see you later, sis," he called, shooting Shannen a look over his shoulder.

A you-lose look, Shannen thought furiously. A triumphant ha-ha look.

Lauren didn't look back at all.

What should she do? Shannen wondered. Would Lauren be terribly upset if Shannen chased after them? Shannen was torn. She glanced up and saw Lucy eyeing her with sympathy.

"Hey, hon, why don't you join us in the Tikki Lounge?" Lucy asked. "Ron—you remember him, don't you? We voted him off right after the tribes merged—has a credit card and is buying everybody a round of drinks."

A pity invitation! They thought she couldn't bear to be away from her twin. Never mind that she'd played along to get to the island today. Shannen was humiliated.

"No, thanks," she murmured. "I, uh, don't really remember Ron. Sorry."

"I'm Ron, and it's okay." Ron stepped forward. "Nobody remembered me. I'd love to get better acquainted with you, though. Let me buy you a drink."

Shannen thought how much she didn't want to get better acquainted with Ron or any of the other guys in the group. There was only one man she wanted to become better acquainted with, and that was Ty.

She wondered if she'd made a major mistake by telling him that she wanted to put sex on hiatus. Not that the hiatus was a mistake—she was certain she was right about that— but saying so the moment before she had to leave him might not have been the best timing.

Maybe she should've said a simple good-night and left it at that.

Shannen trudged to her room carrying Lauren's things.

Timing. A crucial element in any game. The timing had been wrong for her and Ty nine years ago, but now…

Timing Is Everything, the saying went. Was it wrong for them all over again?

Ten

Shannen put on her one-size-fits-all West Falls University nightshirt and studied the list of movies available for viewing in the rooms of the resort. For a fee, of course. If she ordered Russell Crowe, would the cost be deducted from her food allowance?

She wasn't tired, and though she wouldn't have minded something to eat, she wasn't about to call room service. After the network decree, there was probably a block on the phones of all *Victorious* guests, anyway. Raiding the little fridge in the room wasn't worth it, either. There was nothing in it she wanted.

All she really wanted was Ty.

And to have Lauren come to their room saying she hated Jed's womanizing guts, that she hadn't slept with him and had never wanted to.

If she were given a choice, whom did she want more, Ty or a Jed-hating Lauren, to appear at her door? Shannen debated her hypothetical options. At least it was something to do.

Ty was her first choice every time.

When she heard a light knock, she opened the door without bothering to look through the peephole. She was sure it was Lauren, of course. Shannen could only hope it wasn't the under-Jed's-spell version of her twin.

Instead, Ty stood in the doorway, holding a bag.

"Room service. This is the alternate version provided by me and the coffee shop. I have sandwiches, fruit and cake. And wine from the infamous Parrot Room," he added, deadpan. "Not to get you drunk, of course, since that might lead to sex, which you've put on hiatus."

Shannen's heart beat very fast and very hard. "What...how..." She couldn't seem to find the words to ask the obvious questions.

"What am I doing here and how did I get here?" Ty supplied them for her, and she nodded mutely.

"I drove the boat over. I simply told the crew I was taking it to the resort. Nobody tried to stop me." His eyes gleamed. "It helped that Clark Garrett is already here and everyone probably assumed he'd asked me to bring something over. But nobody bothered to ask."

Shannen felt an absurd attack of shyness, definitely a first for her. Shy she'd never been. But standing here with Ty, who was looking so virile and gorgeous and oh, so dear, evoked feelings so powerful that she could do nothing but gaze at him.

"Now we get to the 'why I'm here' part." Ty handed her the bag of food. "I came for dinner. We can eat out on the balcony, like last night."

"Ty..." She was warm all over. From blushing from head to toe? "Last night—"

"Don't worry, I'm not expecting tonight to end like last night's little al fresco picnic. Though I'm certainly not objecting if it should."

Ty put his hands on her waist and carefully moved her aside so he could enter the room. "I respect the limits you've set, Shannen." He shut the door, closing them both in the room. "Stupid and unnecessary though they may be."

His arms encircled her, and he smoothed his hands over the length of her back. Just when she thought he would move his hands lower, just as she anticipated him doing so, he released her.

"You're as safe as you want to be with me, Shannen. Always." He kissed the top of her head. "Now let's eat."

Shannen watched him walk toward the balcony. She gulped for air as a sharp stab of desire pierced her to the core. It would be so easy to suspend her new rule, to lie down on the bed with Ty and make love with him. He was here, she was in love with him, and he wanted her.

After all, they had known each other for nine years. Never mind that she'd had no contact with him from age seventeen to twenty-six and that technically they weren't strangers. Especially not after last night.

She walked to the balcony and stood nervously on the threshold. "I'm in my nightshirt," she murmured, glancing down at the blue-and-white shapeless bag she wore. Wishing it were an eye-popping little number from Victoria's Secret.

"I ought to get dressed."

"Don't bother on my account." Ty grinned wickedly, then added, "Why not just stay comfortable in that? Keep in mind I've seen you in far less every day on the island. Those skimpy little tops and shorts you wore, that sexy bikini of yours... My brain short-circuited every time I looked at you—which was all the time. It was all I could do to remember to keep my camera rolling."

"Cortnee's bikini was much scantier than mine," Shannen protested weakly.

"I never noticed. You were the only one who interested me, Shannen. You still are. Now come out here and eat."

Trembling, Shannen went to him.

Two hours later, they were still out on the balcony, the food completely consumed, the second bottle of wine down to the last drop.

A light breeze from the sea broke the tropical night heat, a full moon lit a pathway in the ocean, but Shannen was oblivious to their physical surroundings. She could've been in a dank cave and she wouldn't have minded, as long as Ty was with her.

They talked and laughed, conversing as comfortably as old friends one minute, then switching to the intoxicating seductive manner of new lovers. Shannen felt an ease she'd never felt with anyone but Lauren, combined with an excitement she'd never experienced with any man. And a desire for him stronger than anything she'd ever known.

It was an irresistible blend, and she wondered if Ty felt the same way.

She should ask him, Shannen decided giddily. Why not? She trusted him enough to ask the question and to hear the answer.

"Ty?" She stood up, and the balcony suddenly took a precarious lurch. She grabbed onto the back of a chair for support.

Ty quickly supplied support of his own. "Uh-oh." He wrapped his arms around her waist, bringing her back against his chest. "Maybe we shouldn't have knocked off that second bottle of wine."

"I'm fine. Just a little light-headed." She looked up at the stars, which seemed to have turned into fireworks, exploding before her eyes. "Maybe very light-headed."

"Into bed you go, Ms. Cullen." Ty scooped her up and carried her inside.

"Ty, I have something to tell you." Shannen linked her

arms around his neck and snuggled against him. "I'll suspend the hiatus for this one night."

Laughing softly, Ty put her on the bed. "You're going to sleep, Shannen. And I'm heading back to camp." He started to tuck the sheet around her. "Good night, baby."

Shannen's fingers fastened around his wrists. "I decided I don't mind if you call me 'baby' every now and then. But only when we're alone."

"Duly noted," agreed Ty. He attempted to disentangle his wrists from her grip, but she held on fast.

"Don't you want me, Ty?" The thought suddenly struck her, and she lacked the control to keep from blurting it out. At this moment she also lacked the inhibition to be horrified by it.

"You know I do, Shannen."

He leaned down to kiss her hungrily, letting her know how much he wanted her. His hands cupped her face, holding her mouth firmly under his as he slanted his lips over hers, drinking deeply from the moist warmth within. His tongue moved provocatively against hers in an erotic, arousing simulation.

Pure liquid pleasure flooded her. She was aware only of Ty and the thrilling mastery of his lips and his hands. Lost in the head-spinning world of sensation, Shannen was completely unprepared for him to lift his mouth from hers.

She watched in confusion as he slowly straightened.

"I didn't come here to get you drunk and take you to bed, Shannen." His voice was husky, his smile roguishly sexy. "I don't *need* to get you drunk to get you into bed. But I do want you to be sure that we know each other well enough, so making love is officially on hiatus until then."

Shannen felt a fierce yearning swelling inside her, so intense she could hardly breathe.

"We know each other well enough, Ty," she whimpered urgently.

Ty walked to the door as if she hadn't spoken at all. He

opened it and paused in the doorway. "When you're stone-cold sober and say those words, we'll make love, Shannen. But you're not, so we won't. Good night, my love."

Sunlight poured into the room through the open curtains, making it literally bright as day.

Automatically, Shannen put her hands over her eyes to block out the light. Closing the drapes after Ty had put her to bed last night hadn't even crossed her mind.

She heard a hoarse moan from the other side of the bed.

"What time is it?" Lauren asked groggily, putting a pillow over her face to shut out the sunlight.

Shannen sat up and looked at the clock. "Five to six. That's a.m.," she added gingerly.

"Is that all?" Lauren wailed. "No wonder I feel so wrecked! I *have* to get some more sleep." She flopped over onto her stomach and buried her face in the pillow.

"I didn't hear you come in last night, Lauren," Shannen said. Or if she had, she didn't remember it.

Shannen vividly recalled her last memory of the night. It was of Ty kissing her senseless and then leaving her, her blood roaring in her ears, her body taut and wet.

His words sounded in her head as a narrative for the visual pictures playing in her mind. *I don't* need *to get you drunk to get you into bed.* No, she'd proved that beyond all doubt.

When you're stone-cold sober and say those words, we'll make love, Shannen. But you're not, so we won't. He had been noble again. Shannen clenched her teeth in frustration.

Noble and outrageously confident. Of course, why shouldn't he be, when she'd practically pleaded with him to go to bed with her? When she'd rescinded her ban on sex less than three hours after making it!

"Ohhhh!" Shannen groaned.

"My thoughts exactly," Lauren replied through gritted teeth.

* * *

"I don't think we're the type for living luxurious lives of leisure, Lauren." Shannen closed her book. "Having all this time on my hands with nothing to do is driving me crazy. At least when we were back on the island, we were always foraging for food. It kept us busy."

"We're doing something, we're reading," said Lauren, not looking up from her book. The cover was a frightening pair of eyes staring demonically at the silhouette of a cowering victim. Knives and droplets of bright blood completed the picture.

The sisters had gone to the gift shop earlier to buy paperbacks to read. Lauren remembered the thousand dollars they'd gained by not eating in the reward contest, money Shannen had completely forgotten about.

Shannen chose a historical romance and expected Lauren to select one in a similar vein. Those were their favorites, but Lauren had bluntly declared she wanted a page-turning thriller, grisly and gory, with a high body count. She'd read every book jacket until finally finding the most horrific. Shannen hated having it in the room with them; it seemed to emit bad vibes.

Or maybe that was Lauren emitting those vibes, because she'd been uncharacteristically difficult since they'd been awakened too early by the morning sun.

Lauren refused to walk on the beach or go to the pool. She wouldn't leave their room for breakfast, lunch or dinner, either. Shannen brought her food from the coffee shop, staying within the daily allowance, and the sisters ate together on the balcony.

Worst of all, Lauren completely clammed up when Shannen asked why she didn't want to leave the room except to buy her gruesome tome of terror. When Shannen casually mentioned Jed's name, Lauren exploded, insisting she never wanted to hear it again. Or the names of any of the other *Victorious* contestants. In fact, she never wanted to talk about the game and the time they'd spent on the island for as long as they lived.

Which ruled out speculating on who would get voted off the island today and who would be the Final Two. Shannen pictured Ty filming it all and silently speculated with herself.

Then she went back to her book, reading until she was stiff from sitting. She stood up and leaned against the balcony railing, gazing at the white sand on the beach and the vast expanse of ocean. The water looked aqua in the sunset. At noon it had been a deeper blue.

Shannen tried to guess which direction the *Victorious* island was. And she thought of Ty again. She'd relived last night in her head over and over, remembering how much she enjoyed being with him. The talking, the laughing, the kissing...

She swallowed hard. She missed him, she wanted to be with him. It was too much to hope that he would come back to the hotel again tonight after the day's filming was through. He simply couldn't keep taking the crew boat to go where he pleased; she knew that, too.

Resignedly she sat back down and picked up her book. The heroine was at that stage of holding off the advances of the hero, whom she claimed to loathe but subconsciously lusted for.

"Stop giving the poor guy such a hard time, Jacinda," Shannen muttered to the girl in the book. "You know you're going to surrender in the end." She gave up and laid it aside. "How's your book, Lauren?"

"Excellent! Another clueless jerk just got offed," exclaimed Lauren ruthlessly.

Now Lauren was rooting for the killer. Shannen walked inside the room to check the clock. How could it only be a few minutes past seven o'clock? This day had gone on for years! And the evening loomed endlessly ahead.

When a knock sounded an hour later, Shannen made a

quick stop at the mirror before answering the door. She pulled her hair out of the ponytail and fluffed it with her fingers. Her striped tank top and navy shorts were a definite improvement over the shapeless nightshirt she'd worn last night.

She admitted to herself that though she'd tried all day to pretend otherwise, she was expecting Ty. After all, he'd shown up unannounced twice before. Still, just in case, she warned herself to be braced for disappointment as she peered through the peephole.

And was not disappointed. She flung open the door.

"Surprise," said Ty. "Or not."

"You're three for three!" Shannen exclaimed, throwing her arms around him and hugging him tight.

Conveniently he had no food or wine tonight and his arms were free to pick her up. She wrapped her legs around his waist and their lips met in passionate fusion.

This was no tentative, preliminary kiss. His tongue entered her mouth and probed intimately, and she responded with an urgency and need that matched his. Instantaneously they were swept into fiery passion, their emotional connection so strong and so natural there could be no denying it.

However, they were not alone.

"To think I thought today couldn't get any worse." Lauren's voice, sardonic and cross, made her presence known. "Ha! The laugh is on me, because it just did. I landed the dreaded role of unwanted third wheel."

Shannen stiffened and Ty tensed. Their private little interlude had come to an abrupt end. She wriggled to be free, and he let her go, though he held her tightly against him, turning the release into a long, slow body caress. Both reluctantly stepped apart.

"Hello, Lauren," he said with commendable geniality. "How are you?"

"Not overjoyed to be playing chaperon," she replied baldly. "If you two want to be alone, you'll have to go

somewhere else. I'm not being driven out of my room."
She purposefully stretched across the bed on her stomach,
her book in front of her face.

"Let's take a walk, Shannen," suggested Ty. "Unless
you'd rather stay here?"

"A walk sounds good." Shannen grabbed his hand and
fairly dragged him from the room. "We've been cooped
up in there most of the day," she confided as they strolled
along the long corridor. "Lauren's...in kind of a mood."

"Tactfully stated." Ty grinned. "Want to know who
was voted off the island?"

"That's how you got the boat again. You offered to bring
the loser over!"

"I didn't offer, I said I was going to do it. Rico is checking into his room right now."

"Rico!" exclaimed Shannen. "How did that happen?"

"Whoever caught the first fish would win the immunity
contest. Konrad had a tug on his pole and immediately
handed it to Cortnee. Sure enough, there was a fish on the
line, which made her the first to catch one."

"So she won immunity. That is, Konrad gave it to her,"
Shannen amended, surprised. "That's unexpected, isn't
it?"

"Nobody saw it coming. Cortnee and Konrad cut their
little deal out of camera range. They both voted Rico off,
but he took it like a good sport."

"And Konrad and Cortnee are the two finalists." Shannen didn't care. She and Ty were together, headed toward
the beach on a beautiful tropical night. Whoever won the
Victorious game, she felt like the *truly* victorious one.

They held hands and walked along the beach together.

"I'm guessing that things didn't go well for Lauren and
Jed?" Ty asked. "She didn't look or sound like someone
who'd spent the day in romantic paradise."

Shannen appreciated the opening. She guessed that Ty
couldn't care less about the alleged Lauren-Jed relationship,

but he knew *she* did. And he was willing and ready to let her confide in him.

They walked and talked for a long time. After exhausting the topic of Lauren and Jed, they moved on to others. Sometimes they paused to discreetly steal a kiss; they were never not touching, either holding hands or wrapping their arms around each other's waists. It was a blissful idyll that neither wanted to end.

But after running into some of the *Victorious* contestants well past midnight, Shannen and Ty recognized it was time to call it a night. They declined the invitation to "join the gang," and Ty walked Shannen back to her room.

"This is kind of like an old-fashioned courtship," he said dryly. "Leaving you at your door with a chaste good-night kiss, my whole body aching with frustration."

"Who said the good-night kiss has to be chaste?" teased Shannen, and initiated a kiss that was anything but.

"Now I'm not only aching with frustration, I'm burning up with it." Ty held her tight, waiting, hoping for the tension to drain from his body. "Shannen, I wanted to tell you—I'm thinking of using the name Howe again."

His tone was deliberately casual, but she was too attuned to him not to know his family name was something he could never be casual about.

"I think it's a good idea, Ty. You're not the one who disgraced it. I think you're going to be the one to make it a name to be proud of again."

"Thanks for the vote of confidence. I hope so. But it won't be as a cameraman, Shannen." He leaned back and gazed down into her warm blue eyes. "If I resumed my law career, I'd take clients who needed me as an advocate but couldn't afford to pay exorbitant attorney fees. I don't want to practice law to become rich and famous."

"Good!" Shannen said succinctly. "There are already too many lawyers like that."

"Anyway, if I opened a law office, it could be anywhere

I wanted to live. That's an option a network cameraman doesn't have."

Shannen nodded, shaky with excitement. Was he trying to say something she hadn't dared dream of?

If so, he never got the chance. Unexpectedly Lauren opened the door. Shannen and Ty, partially leaning against it, were thrown off balance and nearly fell into the room.

"Shannen, I feel like Gramma flashing the front light on and off when we stayed out on the porch too long back in high school," scolded Lauren. "She wanted to go to bed and couldn't, as long as we were out there. Well, I can really relate to that now. Say good-night already and come inside."

Shannen grimaced. "You even sound just like Gramma, Lauren."

"Good night already," Ty quoted lightly and touched Shannen's cheek with his fingertips. "Tomorrow, sweetheart."

The ten contestants who'd been previously ousted filed into the tribal council area, which was lit by hundreds of candles and tall flaming torches placed strategically to ensure the best camera lighting.

Ty waited for Shannen, who was one of the last to come in. She was followed by Lauren and last of all Rico.

Surprisingly, both twins were dressed alike in pale-pink sundresses. Their hair was styled exactly the same way, too, pulled back into a neat thick French braid. They looked like duplicates of each other, though Ty still knew which was Shannen. He just knew.

He also knew that the twins hadn't dressed alike during the entire Victorious shoot. Shannen had confided they'd stopped wearing identical clothing in elementary school unless they were plotting a switch.

Ty was curious and kept his eyes fixed on Shannen, willing her to look at him, to provide even a hint of a clue.

But she never made eye contact with him. Was she avoiding doing so?

It was as if they were back in the early days of *Victorious,* when Shannen had pretended she didn't know who he was, when she'd resolutely followed the game's guidelines "to treat the cameras and crew as if they weren't there."

"Can you believe it? This is our last night of filming!" Heidi whispered to him.

Ty brightened, drawing an odd look from Heidi, who was visibly saddened that the shoot was over. Now she would have to find another job on another show, the fate of production assistants when production wrapped.

Of cameramen, too. But he was an ex-cameraman after tonight. A kind of bittersweet relief surged through Ty. He felt like a refugee who'd decided to return to his native country after a self-imposed exile.

The jury was seated on a three-tiered riser with four of the ex-contestants on each bench. Shannen, Lauren, Rico and Jed sat on the lowest one. Ty noted that Shannen was seated next to Jed, which he knew wouldn't please her. But she'd made the sacrifice to spare Lauren from sitting there.

He wondered if he and Shannen would ever know what, if anything, had transpired between Lauren and Jed, and conceded that basically he didn't care.

Both twins tried to extend the coverage of the very short skirts of their pink dresses over their thighs, the struggle faithfully filmed by Reggie. Despite a valiant attempt, a major expanse of their slim, tanned legs remained exposed.

Ty drew in a deep breath. This was going to be a long night.

Konrad and Cortnee entered next, with Bobby Dixon between them. He motioned the two finalists toward two high-backed chairs. The pair took possession of their jungle thrones, and Bobby began to talk.

"As you know, this is our last night here on the island,

and the winner of *Victorious* will be crowned tonight. We have assembled a jury along with the surviving two contestants in the game.'' Bobby varied his inflections, perhaps in an attempt to create suspense?

If so, he was not succeeding. Ty was bored. He commiserated with the viewing audience who would have to endure the speech.

''Konrad, Cortnee, it's time for each of you to address the jury and tell us why you should be the one voted Victorious. Who wants to go first?'' challenged Bobby.

If he was trying to start a conflict, it didn't work.

''She can go first,'' said Konrad.

''Really? 'Cause I don't mind if you do, Konrad,'' replied Cortnee.

Bobby looked vexed. ''All right, all right, go ahead, Cortnee.''

Cortnee jumped to her feet and gave a perky little speech about the fun she'd had and how much she'd learned during the game. She ended by saying she would like to win, but if her good friend Konrad was the winner, that would be okay with her.

It was Konrad's turn and he remained seated, holding a piece of paper in front of him. He began to read the same speech Cortnee had given, though there was nothing remotely perky in his delivery. He read in a monotone and replaced his name with hers in the appropriate place, but otherwise it was verbatim. Clearly a collaborative effort, with the actual writing undoubtedly done by Cortnee.

Bobby heaved a sigh, displeased by the lack of both drama and suspense. Ty saw the beleaguered announcer glance at Clark Garrett, who stood a few feet away from him. He saw Clark nod his head twice. Two emphatic nods.

Some sort of code? Ty was pondering that when Bobby started talking again.

''I guess everybody remembers that in the past, certain reality shows followed a format from beginning to end.

After the two finalists in the game told us why they should be voted for, each member of the jury would ask a question to be answered by the Final Two.''

Ty panned to the jury members, who were listening intently…or at least giving the impression they were.

"Those questions usually were versions of 'What have you learned about people as a result of being on this show?' or 'What is the most important quality a winner of this game should have?' Am I right?'' Bobby whirled around to face the jury, a move so unexpected a few of them gasped.

"Expect the unexpected!'' Bobby proclaimed. "Because from now on, we're blazing our own trail. After the questioning on those other shows, everybody on the jury would then vote on who they thought should get the money. The votes were read and the winner crowned. But here on *Victorious,* it's going to be different. Because we're different. We are no blatant rip-off of any other show. We're *original!*''

"Bobby's a better actor than I ever thought,'' Heidi murmured to Ty. "He sounds like he actually believes *Victorious* isn't a blatant rip-off.''

There were guffaws among the crew, including Ty.

"We're going to have one final contest to determine the winner,'' Bobby announced, sounding more and more like a carnival huckster. "In the unlikely event of a tie, we'll use the standard method of tiebreaking—that is, the contestant who's already accrued the most votes against them will lose.''

The jury members were talking among themselves. Some appeared annoyed, probably because there would be no TV camera time for them in light of Bobby's declaration.

Ty was a bit perplexed himself. Until this moment the crew had been told the game would be played out in the exact way Bobby had outlined just before repudiating the plan.

"Will our twins, Shannen and Lauren Cullen, please come over here?" Bobby asked, but it was really an order.

The twins exchanged confused glances, which Ty filmed while Reggie captured Konrad's and Cortnee's reactions. The two finalists appeared equally baffled.

"Come on, girls," urged Bobby when neither twin moved. "You see, *you're* the final contest! To win this game, Cortnee and Konrad are going to have to tell you apart. Not unreasonable, since you spent so much time together, true?"

The twins looked appalled. Shannen finally looked directly at Ty, sending him a "Did you know this was coming?" glare. He was glad to be able to honestly shrug his shoulders and shake his head no.

Bobby walked over to the twins, clearly ready to pull them from the risers if they didn't get up of their own accord. Perhaps sensing his determination, Shannen and Lauren rose together and reluctantly followed Bobby to stand in front of Cortnee and Konrad.

Shannen opened her mouth to speak, but before she could say a word, Bobby jumped in with, "No talking, girls. Just stand there and stare into space."

"It's not enough we're the freak show, but we're supposed to stand here like a pair of dummies, too?" complained Lauren, sounding so like Shannen that even Ty had to look twice to make sure it wasn't.

No, it was definitely Lauren who'd spoken.

Bobby frowned his displeasure at the display of disobedience. "Cortnee, Konrad, here are your pens and cards. Write down which twin is standing on the left. For one million dollars, is it Lauren or Shannen?"

Ty was surprised to actually feel suspense build. Winning a million dollars for telling a set of twins apart was definitely a departure from the formula. A rather stupid departure, in his opinion, but if Clark and Bobby wanted the game to end differently from those past shows, they'd succeeded in that regard.

It was too bad both Shannen and Lauren looked ready to commit mayhem for having their identities turned into a contest.

"Time's up!" cried Bobby. "Konrad, what is your answer? Who is the twin on the left? Hold up your card."

Konrad held up the card on which he'd printed "Shannen." "She's the one who mouths off," he said admiringly.

It was Cortnee's turn. She held up her card, which read "Lauren." "Just a guess," she said hopefully.

Bobby paused for heightened dramatic effect. And then: "Cortnee, you are victorious!"

Cortnee screamed and jumped up and down and hugged Konrad and the twins and even Bobby.

"It's like she won Miss Teenage America or something," Jed said disparagingly.

Ty recorded it. He also filmed Konrad saying, "I'm glad for Cortnee. She deserved to win. I got the second prize, and a hundred grand is nothing to whine about."

Finally, Ty recorded the twins' reaction when Bobby asked if they really minded being turned into a guess-their-identities contest.

"Yes," they said together, and glowered at him.

"We're happy Cortnee won, though," Shannen added. "She is so cute and she's going to be a big star."

The filming was through, and the production assistants set to work dismantling the tribal council area. Ty had to push his way through the throng of contestants and crew to finally reach Shannen.

Before he could say a word, Cortnee joined them. "Cute dress, Shannen!" she exclaimed enthusiastically. "Silk, too, huh?"

"We should've known Clark Garrett was up to something when he insisted that Lauren and I buy new dresses— at network expense—in the hotel shop. Then he practically begged us to dress exactly alike." Shannen rolled her eyes. "He said it would be 'good television.' We said no until that snake Jed slithered over and said he agreed with us and we shouldn't listen to Clark."

"That took care of that," Ty interjected wryly. "Lucky for Clark, you and Lauren wouldn't go along with anything Jed suggested."

"We were duped." Shannen was disgusted. "Clark also said the network was buying everybody new clothes to wear tonight, and that turned out to be a lie. It was just Lauren and me for his dumb plan to use us. Sorry, Cortnee. Though I really am glad that you won," she added.

"As soon as Bobby said what the contest was, I knew I'd win," Cortnee said happily. "I learned to tell you and your sister apart after Lauren started hating me. She'd shoot me these drop-dead looks, but you never did, Shannen."

Cortnee glanced from Ty to Shannen. "Now that the game is over, care to tell me what's going on between you two?"

"Us?" Shannen and Ty said at the same time.

"Konrad told me about that day in the ocean when the camera was turned off and it was more than obvious you two knew each other well. He asked if we should use it against you, but I said no." Cortnee smiled shrewdly. "We'd gotten Jed kicked off, and we might come across as mean and nasty if it looked like we were plotting against someone else—especially a twin. I told Konrad we had to think of our images for potential product endorsements. He saw my point."

"Cortnee, you have the instincts of a marketing genius, packaged in a Britney Spears body. I predict you'll go far." Ty laughed.

"I hope so," said Cortnee. "Clark just told me there's a list of agents waiting to contact me. I'll make sure Konrad and Rico get some good deals, too. They're kinda like the brothers I never had, even though I never *wanted* brothers."

"You're sweet, Cortnee," said Shannen. "And whatever your reasons, thanks for—for keeping our secret."

"Which you're not going to tell me, not even now?" Cortnee looked disappointed.

"We'll send you an invitation to our wedding," said Ty. He caught Shannen's hand. "Think we can find a private place where I can propose?"

"I…I think you just did. Indirectly. You…you invited Cortnee to our wedding!"

Shannen was dazed as he pulled her along after him, away from the cast and crew, through the jungle path to the place where they'd first kissed what seemed like eons ago.

"Cortnee said that Konrad told her it was more than obvious that we knew each other well," Ty said, taking Shannen in his arms. "Do you agree that we *do* know each other well?"

"If we don't now, I expect we'll know each other very well by the time of our wedding." Shannen smiled up at him, her blue eyes shining with laughter and love.

"So you're accepting my proposal?"

"Actually you haven't officially made one yet, Ty."

"I'll correct that oversight immediately." Ty got down on bended knee and took her hand. "Shannen, will you marry me?"

"Yes, I will, Ty." She knelt down beside him. "I love you, Ty. I love you so much."

"And I love you, Shannen. I fell in love with you nine years ago and I'm still in love with you." He took her mouth in a long, lingering kiss filled with love and passion and commitment.

The emotional intensity shook them both.

"I wish we could be together tonight." Shannen sighed wistfully. "All night, in our own room. But Clark said the crew is staying here in the camp tonight."

"They are. But I'm going to the hotel with you—and we're definitely getting our own room," promised Ty.

"But, Ty—"

"My time with *Victorious* is over. The editors have the footage, and there is nothing more for me to film. I meant what I said about opening my own law practice, Shannen. I thought it could be in West Falls, if you'd like."

"Where my job and my family are." Shannen was thrilled. "I'd love that, Ty. But we'd better start economizing right away, because it'll take a while to get a law practice established in West Falls. Luckily my job at the hospital will provide us with health benefits, but I really don't think we can afford the five hundred dollars a night for a room at the resort. Maybe we can—"

"There's something else I've been meaning to tell you, Shannen," Ty cut in. "Five hundred dollars for a room is chump change to me. You see, uh, I didn't lose my money. My personal wealth wasn't touched by any of the lawsuits against the other Howes. It can't and never will be."

"You-you're saying that…that—"

"I'm rich. Very rich. Are you angry?" He challenged.

"I'm stunned! Why did you tell me that you'd lost everything?"

"You were the one who said I had money issues, Shannen. And you were right. But now—thanks to you—I no longer have them. At least as far as you're concerned."

He kissed her deeply. And kept a firm hold on her, locking his eyes with hers.

"You're not even going to let me get mad because you didn't trust me enough to tell me the truth, are you?" she asked in the testy tone familiar to *Victorious* viewers.

"That's the plan." He kissed her again. "I do trust *you,* Shannen. And I fully intend to use my money to buy your goodwill. You couldn't stay too mad at a guy who pays for the repairs to the family diner and Gramma's roof and sets

Jordan and Josh up in the landscaping business of their dreams, could you?''

''You remembered all that, even Josh's and Jordan's names,'' Shannen marveled.

''I also know the names of their two kids, if you care to quiz me. Everything you told me about you and your family is worth remembering, Shannen. What's important to you is important to me, too.''

''How could I ever stay mad at a guy like that?'' Shannen murmured in a warm, tender tone familiar only to those she loved.

''How could you?'' agreed Ty.

And holding hands, they went to find the boat that was leaving the island.

*   *   *   *   *